The Forest

L. K. Tamaya

For Penny

CONTENTS

ONE

The hall floor creaked. The thin sliver of light beneath the door flickered then went dim. I held my breath, hoping she hadn't heard too much.

"It's time to go sleep now, okay?" Mum's voice was muffled through the door, but if I could hear her, she could certainly hear me. I should have been more careful.

"Okay," I said, in my sleepiest sounding voice.

"I mean it," Mum went on. "No more radio. It's past ten, and you've got school tomorrow."

I snuggled down into my duvet. I could tell by the tone of her voice that she wasn't really cross. "Okay, sorry."

"Good. Goodnight then."

"Goodnight." I closed my eyes. "And goodnight," I whispered into the empty room.

TWO

I woke to a cool, golden dawn and a stomach full of jelly. It was going to be a great day, and just the thought of seeing my friends was enough to get me moving, even after a whole summer of lie-ins.

I steeled myself for the cold air, then pulled back the bedclothes and slid out onto the carpet. My hair was tangled and in my face, but I could hear the shower running in the next room. Mum was already in there; I'd have to wait.

My new school bag sat on the desk, already full of all the things I'd need today and tempting me to go through them one more time. I needed to check I had everything anyway, I told myself. I pulled it closer and opened the top. Pencil case, books, paper, hairbrush and the tiny make-up bag I'd gotten for my birthday, complete with lip gloss and blusher, all ready to go. Just looking at it all made me itch to get on with the day. My stomach was so wriggly I wondered if I'd be able to eat my breakfast, and I had to take a deep breath and tell myself to get a grip.

The shower sputtered to a dribble, then stopped. The bathroom door clicked open. I pulled my towel off the radiator and had just reached for the door knob when I hesitated. Had something moved behind me? With a glance over my shoulder, I could see that nothing was out of place, and I grinned. Then I raised a hand, waved at the empty room and slipped into the hallway, eager to get ready and out the front door.

Mum dropped me off at my new school on her way to work –for my first day only –and within five minutes I was chatting with three friends from my old school as we headed off for registration. There were so many more kids at this school and it was so much bigger than my last one that I kept getting lost in the corridors. But it was more exciting than frightening, and together we all managed to find the right rooms until lunchtime. That morning went so quickly I found myself eating lunch before I'd even caught my breath.

It was a lovely autumn day, still warm and bright, and we decided to sit outside to eat our sandwiches and watch one of the school teams practicing on the fields.

"What did you do all summer?" Emily asked. She was sunning herself on the grass next to me, shading her eyes with a tanned hand while crowds of boys ran up and down the pitch in front of us.

"Hmm?" I turned to her out of my day dream. "Oh, not much."

Emily grinned at me then glanced up at the boys. I felt my cheeks turning hot. I knew exactly what she was thinking, and I didn't want to go there.

"What did you do?" I asked her, instead of answering.

Emily shrugged. "We went on holiday to France for two weeks, it was okay. Dad made us look at lots of museums." She made a face and turned to Holly. "At least I got a tan though. What about you, Hol?"

Holly chuckled as she pushed her glasses up her nose. "I

met up with Javier," she said. "It was okay."

I pushed myself up off the grass to stare at her. "Okay? It sounds better than okay to me. I can't believe you met up with him! How did you manage it?"

A grin spread across her face. "I convinced Mum to invite him back for a few weeks, because it had really helped my Spanish."

We all laughed. I shook my head at her; I couldn't believe how she got away with this stuff.

"You're unbelievable," Emily said. "I wish I could convince my mum to invite someone that cute to stay with us."

"The only boys I saw were Mikey and Toady," I said, rolling my eyes.

"I knew you'd seen him," Emily said, turning to point a finger at me. "You can't tell me you don't fancy him."

"You know I can't stand Toady." I had hoped she would forget all about him over the summer. Emily thought my cousin was extremely cute, even though he was a complete prat. "And he's my cousin. Yuck!"

"Did you have to stay at your aunts?" Holly asked, breaking up the argument before it could get going.

"No, but Mum was too busy to do much and I had a job at the shop with Milly, so the only kids I saw all summer were my cousins."

"At least you made some money," Emily said, taking a long slurp from her juice. "I can't believe your mum let you get a job. My dad keeps saying not till I'm fifteen."

I couldn't help grinning. "I know, it's really cool. And she said I can keep doing it on weekends so long as I don't mess up at school. Only after I get settled in here, of course."

"What are you going to do with all the money?" Holly asked.

I shrugged. "I dunno, put it in the bank I suppose."

Emily sighed. "You're nuts – I'd be buying loads of makeup and stuff with it!"

"Yeah, but you're a bimbo!" I said, pulling a face. We all burst into giggles.

Lunch finished too quickly. The bell hurried us out of the sunshine and back into the classrooms before we'd even caught up on everyone's summer. But, for that first day at least, I didn't mind; it was so exciting to be starting at a new school.

By the time the last bell went I was wondering if every day was going to be so busy and exhausting. All I could think about was getting home and having some dinner, but I still had homework to finish before I could curl up in front of the TV.

At the gates, Holly hurried off to meet her dad, and Emily and I headed off together.

"Mum was dead set on picking me up," Emily said. She hefted her bag a little higher on her shoulders. "I told her no way!"

"You're lucky," I said. "My mum'll be at work until at least seven."

She shook her head. "You're the one who's lucky. I'd love to have the house to myself."

Emily had four brothers and sisters, and her house was never quiet. She couldn't understand why I got fed up of being home on my own. I sighed.

"I can't believe how much homework they gave us."

"I know, you'd have thought they'd give us the first night off!"

We both shook our heads. All those new books were exhausting to carry.

"I suppose they want us to take it really seriously," I said. "Like it matters how we do at school now."

"I know," Emily said. "I mean, if we were sixteen I could

understand it, but did you see Mrs Richardson going on about our end of year exams?" She snorted.

I laughed too, and we plodded on down the road. The weather was still warm and my bag was uncomfortably heavy on my back. I could feel my shirt getting damp in the heat and sticking to my skin, and my keys were pulling at my trouser pocket.

It took us ten minutes to get to Emily's road, but we didn't talk about much other than all our new teachers and which ones were the best. I waved goodbye to Emily at the crossing, promising to meet her there the next morning. Then I set off for home. It was another 20 minute walk over the bridge and past my aunt's deli, back to my empty house.

We had all agreed during the summer that I was old enough to be at home by myself now that I was at secondary school, so I didn't have to spend my afternoons with Sandy and my cousins anymore. This was both a good and a bad thing. Good, because Toady, my 16 year old cousin, was a big pain. And the little one, Mikey, was sweet but really annoying.

But it was bad too, because Milly, who was two years above me at school, was my best friend and I didn't get to see her much apart from when I was at the shop because she helped her mum so much. My aunt hadn't been well for years, and Milly was always doing something or other for her, or taking care of Mikey.

None of them were outside when I passed, so I carried on down the road, around the corner and past the little park to our house, where it stood almost right on the pavement. Getting my keys out from where they'd been pulling at my pocket, I headed up the steps and unlocked the door.

Inside the house, I breathed a big sigh of relief and dumped my bag in the hall. It was quiet in here. No matter what I might say to my friends, it was kind of cool to be home all alone, free to do whatever I wanted. I knew I had at least 3 hours until Mum came home. More than enough time to have something to eat, do my homework and chill out in front of the TV for a bit, watching whatever I liked.

Our house was small and quite old, but it was beautiful and decorated in all sorts of interesting things Mum had found through her work. There were old statues, strange paintings, faded wall hangings and odd, carved wooden chests and tables in every room. It was tidy, but most people thought it was cluttered – that was just because they didn't understand how lovely everything was.

I took two minutes to make myself a sandwich, then headed for my favourite window seat to watch the birds fighting over peanuts in our tiny garden.

"Hi, Anne."

I nearly fell off my seat. Gulping down my mouthful of sandwich, I turned around, but there was no one there. I relaxed again.

"Phew," I said, waving at the empty room and then picking up my sandwich for another bite. "You scared me."

"I'm sorry," said the voice, so close that if I'd been able to see its owner they'd have been sitting right beside me. "Who did you think it was?"

I shrugged. "Some crazy person who'd gotten into the house without me knowing?" I laughed. It was hard to get used to speaking to a disembodied voice. Trying to decide whether it sounded more like a man or a woman had done my nut in for weeks, but I'd had all summer to get used to it by now. "But it's just you."

"Yep, just me. How did your first day at school go?"

I nodded and swallowed my mouthful. "Good. It was fun."

"That's good. Were your friends there?"

"Uh huh."

"I bet you had lots of fun together."

I nodded.

"So what's the plan for this afternoon?" the voice said, and I sighed.

"I've got homework to do."

"No way – already?"

"Yep."

"That's not fair."

"Tell that to my teachers," I said. "We can talk later though."

There was a brief pause, then the voice said, "Sure."

I grabbed my plate and ducked into the kitchen to leave it on the sideboard.

"Speak to you later then," I called over my shoulder, heading for the stairs. There was no answer.

My new homework was so much harder than my old stuff. It took me almost until Mum came home to finish it. By the time I heard the front door bang open and her footsteps in the hallway, my head was aching and I was feeling much less excited about my new school.

"Anne?" she called up the stairs, then I heard the rustling as she took off her coat and shoes. I closed my workbook with a long sigh, rubbed my eyes, then got up to meet her.

"Yup," I called back as I came down the stairs. She looked up, and I saw how tired she looked again; her hair was all fuzzy and she had big bags under her eyes. But she smiled when she saw me, and before I'd even reached the bottom step she folded me into a big hug.

"How was your day?" I said, following her into the kitchen.

She shrugged. "It was okay." She flicked on the kettle. "I had a big meeting in London and spent most of the day on trains getting there and back." She flashed me a grin. "How was your day? I was thinking about you."

I grinned, but only half-heartedly, and handed her two plates. She took them, placed them on the side, then turned and smoothed back my hair with a long look.

"It was great," I said, pulling away to get food out of the fridge. "Emily and Holly met me and we have all our classes together."

Mum nodded, turning back to the hob and starting to throw things into the pan. "I'm glad. Maybe you can go and spend some time at Emily's house after school some days? Do your homework together?"

Our dinner began to sizzle and pop and the kitchen filled with the sweet smell of lemon grass. My mouth began to water.

"I think I'll need it," I said, filling up a glass of water and going to sit at the table. "My homework tonight was so hard."

She shot me a sympathetic glance and tipped the steaming vegetables out onto plates. "Here," she said. "You'll feel better for this. And we can have pancakes for desert if you like."

I tried to look pleased – pancakes are my favourite food ever – but the throbbing in my head was even worse and all I could manage was a nod.

Mum frowned at me and put her fork down. "You are tired, aren't you?" she said, reaching out and squeezing my hand. I nodded, focusing on getting the hot food into my mouth.

"Well," she said, sitting back and picking up her fork again, "if you don't object, I think it'll just be a bath and bed after dinner." She smiled at me, looking almost as tired as I felt. "We're a right pair, aren't we? Don't worry – it'll get easier."

I nodded again. I wasn't going to argue with her; I was pooped.

THREE

I didn't dream at all that night, and I woke up in exactly the same position I had fallen asleep in. But I did feel much better after all that sleep, the sun was as bright as it had been the day before, and my cheerful mood had returned. I was up, dressed and downstairs having breakfast before I even heard Mum stir. She got mornings off on Thursdays so she could work on Sundays. It was the only lie in she got, so I was always careful not the wake her up.

I made myself some toast and went to sit in my window seat to watch the sunlight creeping across our little patch of lawn. It was my favourite time of day – so peaceful and quiet, with nothing to worry about and the whole day at my new school to look forward to.

"Good morning," said a voice behind me. This time I didn't jump, but just turned around and smiled.

"Good morning."

There was no one there, but that had stopped seeming strange. I'd been talking to my imaginary friend all summer – almost two months now – and while I knew it was pretty childish and didn't want to admit it, it was nice to have someone to talk to while everyone else was busy.

"And how are you feeling?" the voice asked.

I nodded. "Better. Great," I said, stretching in the warm patch of sunlight from the window.

"We didn't talk last night." I frowned. "Oh yeah, I'm sorry. I was so tired I fell straight asleep."

There was a pause, and then, "I waited for you."

I felt bad at that. "I'm really sorry," I said to the voice, shifting on my seat to see the empty room better. "I was really, really tired. But we can talk now."

I smiled and waiting for the voice to answer. I'd learned over the summer how he could be a little sulky, but it wouldn't last long.

"That's okay," the voice said, and I felt a soft breeze pass my face. "I forgive you."

I laughed and shook my head; he was so funny. "What did you want to talk about, anyway?"

"I just wanted to talk about your day." In my mind's eye, I could see him shrugging.

"There wasn't much to tell – it was fun, but really tiring. I'm looking forward to getting used to it and making some new friends."

"You already have friends."

I hesitated. That was a weird thing to say. "I do," I said, "but..."

"But they don't understand you."

"I don't know what you mean," I said. "They're great friends; we get on really well."

"Yes," said the voice, "but you can't talk to them like you talk to me."

"Well, no," I said, puzzled, "but that's because you're imaginary – it doesn't matter what I say to you."

There was a moment of silence. "Exactly," the voice said, "I'm imaginary, and they're real – so they can't know what it's like to be you, or understand what you're feeling."

I shook my head; I had no idea what he was getting at, but it was silly. Of course my friends understood me. "You're being weird!" I said, laughing.

The voice laughed as well. "I suppose I am, if that's what you think!"

I brushed the toast crumbs off my legs onto the plate, then got up. "I'd better go." I could hear Mum moving around upstairs now. "I don't want Mum to hear me talking to you like the other night. She'll think I'm nuts!"

"We wouldn't want that."

I felt another breath of air against my arm.

"Yeah, if I tell her my imaginary friend's back she'll have me off to the doctors; you're supposed to be for little kids."

"I'm for you, whenever you like," the voice said, and I smiled.

"Okay, well I'll see – I mean, speak to – you later then."

"You bet," the voice said, and I went to put away my breakfast things and get ready for school.

My second day passed even more quickly than the first one. There was so much to remember and figure out; all the teachers were different and had different rules, the campus was huge and felt like a maze, and there were so many other kids I sometimes felt like I was going to get swept away in a flood of them.

Luckily, Emily and Holly were there too. All of our classes were together so we could stick with each other and feel less alone. There were loads of other kids from our old school as well, but they were mostly in different classes, so we hardly saw them. And there were lots of new friends to make, with all the different kids from the surrounding villages. Some of them were pretty normal, like us, but some of them seemed to come from a different planet!

Holly, Emily and I were laughing about some of them on our way home that afternoon when we were passed by Milly and Toady on their bikes.

"Hi," Milly called out. She pulled her bicycle off the road and hopped onto the pavement. Toady rolled his eyes and carried on down the road without her.

I turned to give Milly a hug as Holly and Emily said hi. Then we all carried on down the pavement together, with Milly pushing her bike beside us, all pink from cycling in the sun.

"How's it going?" she asked, scooping her long, dark hair off her back and fanning her neck. We all shrugged.

"It's good," I said.

"Yeah, it's okay," Holly added.

Milly raised her eyebrows. "It's different from middle school, isn't it?"

We nodded at her; our school bags were dragging on our shoulders, and I could feel another headache building already. The day had been fun, but I was beginning to wonder if I'd ever get used to it.

Milly gave me a side-ways hug. "Don't worry about it," she said, "it gets easier. Once you know the ropes, you'll get on fine."

Emily sighed. "I can't imagine that ever happening," she said. "I feel like my head's going to explode – and the homework last night was impossible!"

"Yeah," Holly agreed. "I don't know how you do it; I think I'm going to go crazy."

We all nodded.

"And," Holly said, "we're so small compared with all those

sixth formers – I feel like someone's just going to squish me, like there'll be a stampede or something."

Milly laughed and shook her head. "Everyone feels like that at first; don't worry about it. We all remember what's it's like. And if you really do have problems, tell me and I'll try to figure something out, okay?" Milly swung herself back onto the bike and kicked off into the road.

"Okay," Holly said, giving me and Emily a dark look, "but just you wait – I'll be paté before the end of the week."

"No you won't," Milly called over her shoulder, grinning at us. "You'll be fine."

And she disappeared round the corner.

I smiled; Milly always made me feel better.

"I'd better go too," Holly said, frowning at her watch. "Dad'll be livid."

She headed off in the opposite direction, and Emily and I watched her go.

"Do you think there's any chance he'll even notice she was late?" I said, rolling my eyes.

She grinned back at me. "Nope," she said, "but mine will if I don't get a move on – come on."

We walked on without talking for a while, enjoying the sunshine. I was thinking about my conversation with my imaginary friend that morning. At the time, I hadn't paid much attention to what he'd been saying; it was nonsense. But the idea that nobody really understands each other had been stuck in the back of my head all day, like a catchy song, and something about it was bugging me. I turned the idea over, trying to figure out why I couldn't shake it, before being interrupted.

"What are you thinking about?"

"Oh," I said, feeling my face flush. I didn't want anyone to know I was having conversations with thin air at home.

"Nothing."

She nodded and gave me a sly look. "Yeah, right," she said, nudging me with her elbow. "Were you thinking about a boy?"

She drew the last word out into a drawl and I rolled my eyes.

"No. You are so childish," I said, shaking my head.

She laughed. "Well, what then? You were thinking about something; I could see it."

"I was," I said, hesitating. "Do you think I understand you?"

"What do you mean?"

I shrugged. "I mean – do you think I know how you feel about stuff, I suppose?"

She gave me a little smile, and said, "I suppose so. Yeah. Why?"

"I dunno, just something I was thinking about. I don't know why I thought of it."

She looked at me. "Do you think I understand you?" she asked. But she didn't wait for my answer. "You don't, do you? That's why you thought of it. Why? What have I done?"

"Nothing," I said, wishing I hadn't said anything. "You haven't done anything – I do think you understand me."

"Yeah right," she said, and shook her head. "I could see what you were thinking – you can't lie to me about it now."

I opened my mouth to explain, but couldn't think of way to do it without making myself look like any idiot. Emily caught me hesitating and exploded.

"I don't know why you think you're so special," she said, her voice getting shriller by the minute. "You act like no one else has problems, and none of us are as mature as you. And you're wrong."

I stammered and tried to grab her hand, but she pulled it away.

"I can't believe you! After we've been friends for so long!"

she said, hefting her bag high on her back and picking up her pace.

"You don't understand," I said, trying to stop her long enough to explain.

"No," she shouted back. "Clearly not!"

We were nearly at the road where she lived and she sped up towards the turn. I shouted after her, but she just grabbed her bag harder and walked off as fast as she could without actually running. I wanted to go after her, but my legs felt like jelly. I'd never had a fight with Emily before; we were always such good friends. I didn't know what to do.

Before I could make up my mind to follow her, she disappeared around the corner and it was too late. She'd be at her house in a few minutes, and I didn't want to have to explain about our argument to her mum. And besides, there were other kids on the road, all walking home after school, and some of them were staring at me now. My cheeks burned at their curious glances, and I decided the best thing to do was to get home as quickly as possible and sort it all out tomorrow.

Mum wasn't home when I got there and I had to use my key to get in. I hadn't expected her to be there, but I was still disappointed; I wanted a hug and someone to talk to before I gave in and cried. But there was no point wishing. I'd just have to deal with it on my own until she got home. I dumped my bag in the usual spot and went straight to the kitchen to get something to eat.

"Hello there," said a familiar voice behind me, making me jump.

"Jeezus," I said, turning around with my mouth full of sandwich. "You made me jump. Again."

"How's it going?" he said, and I rolled my eyes.

"Rubbish," I said, sitting down on one of the chairs and

putting my head in my hands. "I had a fight with Emily, and I don't even understand why."

"How upsetting," the voice said. I could feel the strange breeze on my face again as it spoke, and my stomach tightened. Now there were tears in my eyes. I told myself to get it together and wiped them away.

"Sorry," I said, feeling stupid.

"That's perfectly all right," the voice said.

I gave the room a weak smile. "You're really nice," I said. "You know, for someone who's not real."

"Well that's because you're nice!"

I shook my head. "I don't know about that. I think this argument was my fault – I really hurt her feelings."

"What did you do?"

I shrugged, thinking back to earlier. "I dunno. I just asked if she thought I understood her. I don't know why; it had just been in my head all day. And then she asked me the same question…"

"And you said no?"

"No!" I said, shaking my head. "I wouldn't say that. Emily is one of my best friends." I sighed. "Anyway, she got really upset. She said all sorts of nasty things – that I was stuck up and think I'm special and all mature."

I sighed again and took another bite of my sandwich.

"I don't know what to do about it, because I don't really understand why we had a fight in the first place. I don't know what I did wrong!"

There were a few moments of silence while I chewed, thinking it all over again. Then I shook my head and stood up.

"Where are you going?" the voice asked out of the silence.

I crossed to the sink and put my plate on the side. "I'm going to go and do my homework," I said, feeling tired just at the thought of all those books. This school was proving to be far more exhausting and complicated than I'd expected.

"But we're talking," the voice said, and I rolled my eyes.

"Look, I've had enough arguing for one day, okay?"

The was another moment of silence and then the voice spoke again. "Fine," it said, "I'm just trying to help."

Part of me felt bad for a moment, but another part of me was just annoyed. "You're just my imagination; you can't help. Just go away."

There was no answer. I sighed, feeling guilty but also relieved. Shaking my head, I told myself not to be so silly – he was an imaginary friend, and I was way too old to have one of those. I grabbed my bag and climbed the stairs. Behind my eyes, a dull throbbing was making it hard to see. Thinking that I wasn't going to be any good at schoolwork tonight, I took some paracetamol from the bathroom and gulped them down while I set myself up at my desk. Looking at my homework diary, I could tell it was going to be a long evening.

FOUR

"Anne?"

Pain flared through my forehead, then faded. I lifted my head from the desk and blinked in the half-light. "Mum?"

She was standing beside me, illuminated only by the faint glow of dusk through the window. Her hand was pressed to my forehead. "Are you all right, love?" she said, peering at my face.

Sitting up, the headache faded to a faraway throb. I nodded, pushing back my hair and looking down at the workbook I'd been drooling on. "Yeah," I said, "I'm fine. I just fell asleep, that's all."

She nodded, still frowning. Then she stepped back to the bedroom door and turned the hall light on. The brightness hurt my eyes for a moment. I had to blink a few times to stop them from welling with tears.

"Are you hungry?"

"Um, yeah. I think so."

She gestured for me to follow her downstairs, and I got to my feet. My head spun as I stood, but my tummy gurgled too. I really was hungry.

"When did you get home?" I asked, taking the stairs two at a time behind her.

"Just now – I came up to find you when you didn't answer me," she said, catching my eye.

"Sorry, I had a really long day. I must have fallen asleep doing my homework."

"Well, you must have needed it. You were hard to wake up."

She smiled and reached over to put the oven on. I ran my hands over my face, then glanced at the clock. It was just coming up to 7 o'clock, I'd been asleep for nearly two hours. I groaned.

"What's the matter?"

"My homework. I didn't finish it."

She gave me a sympathetic look. "Is there much still to do?"

"Loads."

"Well, only one more day until the weekend – you can finish it then."

I nodded, biting back a sigh; I'd been planning to hang out with Milly most of the weekend, not spend it doing homework. I didn't know how she had so much free time to work in the shop. She must have even more homework than me.

Dinner didn't take long and we were soon at the kitchen table surrounded by the delicious smell of Mum's cooking. I was ravenous, and finished within ten minutes.

Mum caught my eye and laughed. "I think all this hard work is making you hungry," she said. "Why don't you get some ice cream out of the freezer for dessert?"

"Thanks, Mum," I said. I left my plate on the sideboard and grabbed a bowl. "You're the best."

She nodded as if she already knew that and watched me tuck in to a huge helping of raspberry ripple. It didn't take me long to eat it all, and by the time I was finished so was she. I helped her tidy up then headed up the stairs to my bedroom. My head was starting to throb again and I couldn't stop my eyelids from drooping.

"Bed for you, I think," Mum said, putting a hand on my shoulder and steering me towards the bathroom. "Just brush your teeth and get into bed – don't worry about any more homework tonight."

"It's only 8 o'clock,' I said, groaning. I knew she was right, but I felt like a baby going to bed so early.

"And you're falling asleep on your feet." She shook her head and pushed me towards the sink. "Stop fighting it."

She turned back towards the stairs, grabbing a book from the shelf by my door.

"And don't worry, Annie; it'll get easier. I promise."

I nodded, but didn't bother answering. It was much, much easier to just brush my teeth and let myself sink closer and closer to sleep. I knew I'd be out before my head even hit the pillow; there was no room for anything but sleep in my brain. I'd just have to talk to her about Emily tomorrow. And who knew? Maybe it would all just blow over by the morning and everything would be fine again.

FIVE

I had another night of deep, dreamless sleep. But when I woke up in the morning, it wasn't to the sunny feeling of the last few days; I felt grey and sluggish. At the back of my head there was still a throbbing that shouldn't have been there. I rolled over and tried to hide under the covers from the bright sunlight. That kind of beautiful morning just didn't match how I was feeling, and I wasn't in the mood to enjoy it.

My tummy was rumbling, but not just because I was hungry. There was a tightness there too, reminding me just how worried I was about my argument with Emily. Well, I told myself, I'd just have to fix it. There was no reason for us to not be friends; it was just a misunderstanding.

I dragged myself out of the warm bed. The sight of my school bag at my desk was far less welcome than it had been two days ago; I couldn't believe the difference such a short amount of time could make. Now all I could think of was how heavy it looked and how much homework I had left. I rubbed my face hard and took a deep breath, trying to snap out of it. There was nothing I could do about the homework now, so there was no point worrying about it. At least I didn't have to hand any of it in today.

Breakfast was quiet because Mum was already up and on the ' phone in the living room. I forced myself to eat some cereal, swallowing against the thick feeling in my throat. There was no way I'd be able to talk to her before I left for school; she was too busy. I wondered if the imaginary voice would start talking to me – I was on my own, after all – but there was no sign of him. It was probably for the best. I didn't need someone else making me feel guilty, even if they weren't real.

Half seven came before I knew it and I was out the door into the crisp sunshine, loaded up with that rucksack, with Mum pulling the door closed behind us.

"It's a beautiful day again," she said, taking a deep breath and looking up at the trees that towered behind our house. "You're lucky you don't have to be inside all day, missing it all."

I nodded and tried to smile. I knew she was right, and I tried to tell myself there was no reason to feel this miserable, but I couldn't help it. She gave me a quick hug and got in her car, grinned at me, then started the engine. I waved at her, turned, and headed off into town, wondering if Emily would meet me on the way or if she'd get a lift instead.

Mum beeped her horn as she passed me and I watched her disappear around the corner. I couldn't help sighing as I hefted my rucksack higher onto my shoulders. Sometimes, I wished she didn't have to work so much. Or even that she could pass my school on her way to the station. But thinking like that made me feel even worse; it wasn't like she'd planned for things to be like this – I knew that. I just needed to get on with it, I told myself, picking up speed.

The day sucked, just like I'd known it would the moment I woke up. Emily didn't meet me on the way to school, but got a lift with Holly instead. It turned out they'd spent most of the evening talking about me on the phone, getting even more annoyed with me.

What made things even worse was that they refused to even talk to me about it. Instead, they spent the whole day leaving me out so that I had to sit with kids I didn't know in all my classes and spend lunchtime on my own. By the time I left to go home, I was fighting back tears. I just wanted to hide and never go back.

The walk home had never been so tiring. Groups of other kids kept passing me, some of them staring, and I felt like a complete freak. I didn't even see Toady and Milly on their bikes, so I was on my own the whole time. But when I reached the shop, I saw why. Toady was outside on the pavement, smoking a cigarette, and I could make out Milly through the shop door, sweeping.

"Hi," I said, slowing down to talk to him.

He scowled at me. "What do you want?"

I stared back at him. Normally, I wouldn't bother, especially when he was in such a bad mood, but I needed to talk to Milly.

"Can Milly come out?" I asked, glancing over his shoulder.

He shrugged. "Go and ask her yourself." He flicked his cigarette onto the floor and stalked off down the alley at the back of the shop. I watched him go for a minute then headed into the shop.

"Hi," I said, trying to smile as cheerfully as I could. Milly looked tired, but she grinned when she saw me and stood the broom against one of the shelves.

"Hi," she said. She pushed her hair out of her face. "How's it going?"

"S'okay." I said, avoiding her gaze. I pointed upwards, to where they lived above the shop. "What about you? Have you been home all day?"

"Yeah. Mum's worse today, so Toady and I stayed home to look after the shop and stuff."

"Is she okay now?"

"Mum? She'll be all right. Tomorrow probably. It's nothing special."

I nodded again, relieved. I wondered if I should offer to go and see her, but Milly interrupted before I could ask.

"She's asleep now, otherwise you could stay for a bit."

She gave me smile. Anyone else probably wouldn't notice, but I could see how tired and stressed she was. I couldn't even imagine what it would be like if my mum was always sick, and I knew Milly worried if it was bad. I wondered if she minded having to stay home so much. I caught her eye and tried to let her know I understood.

I leaned against a shelf stacked full of flour bags. "What are you doing this weekend?"

Milly shrugged. "I don't know. Probably just hanging around the shop, doing my homework. Do you want to come and do it with me?"

I grinned at her. "Yeah."

She grinned back. "Great. And when we're finished, we could go to the woods, or for a bike ride, if you like?"

The idea felt like a ray of sunshine bursting through my grey day. Finally, something to look forward to.

"I'd better go," I said, glancing up at where I knew her mum was sleeping. I didn't want to get in the way and I knew Milly probably had a hundred things to do before she could go and eat.

Milly nodded and reached for the mop again. "See you tomorrow," she said, leaning on it and giving me a wry wave. I grinned back at her and turned to leave, feeling a million times better. Then I stopped. She was staring at me, her face pale.

"What is it?" I said, looking around to see what she was staring at.

Milly hesitated for a minute, swallowed, then shook her head. "Nothing," she said. "I just thought I saw something, that's all."

"Are you okay?" I asked, stepping closer and reaching out for her shoulder. But she just nodded and stepped back, starting to mop the floor again. "Yeah, I'm just really tired," she said. "So tired I'm seeing things, apparently."

It sounded like she was joking, but her voice was shaking as she said it. I watched her for a few seconds, wondering what to say, then I decided to leave it. She clearly didn't want to talk about it right now.

"Okay," I said, turning to leave again. "Well, go and get some rest then. I'll see you tomorrow?"

She nodded and I headed back out onto the bright street. As I walked away, I looked back over my shoulder, but there was nothing to see in the shop's tinted windows but my own dark reflection.

SIX

My head was hammering by the time I reached my front door. The little ray of sunshine I'd felt with Milly had vanished as quickly as it had appeared. I climbed the steps to the door, jangling my keys and wishing Mum was home. I had never wanted to talk to her so badly before. With all that had happened this week, I really needed to talk to someone. For a moment, I even considered calling my dad, but I dismissed the idea as soon as I thought of it. He was way too busy to speak to me at the moment. And Helen, his new girlfriend, was never pleased to hear from me anyway.

No, I'd just have to wait until Mum got home unless my good, old imaginary friend re-appeared. I snorted at the idea, glad no one else had heard me talking to the voice. In their current mood, Emily and Holly would get a kick out of spreading something like that around school.

The house was cool after the heavy autumn warmth of the street. I made for the kitchen. At least I had two whole days before I had to go back to school; I could finish my homework, talk to Mum and Milly, and hopefully sort everything out with Emily and Holly before Monday came. I poured myself a big glass of water and grabbed a packet of crisps. I wasn't hungry, but Mum always made a big fuss if I didn't eat something after school. I could hear her suggesting I had an apple instead, and rolled my eyes. Then I headed for the TV.

I had all weekend to do my homework, so there was no point in killing myself tonight to get it done. My head was hurting and all I wanted to do was veg out in front of the TV until mum came home. I made myself a nest of cushions on the sofa and sipped my water, pausing before flicking on the set. The house was quiet; no sign of my friendly voice tonight. I wondered where he was, but not for long. The excited voices of a talk show made me wince, and I started flipping through the channels.

It didn't take long for me to relax. I was almost ready to fall asleep when there was a huge bang and then a crash from upstairs. My eyes flew open and I sat up, knocking my glass onto the carpet. The TV was too loud to hear anything. Grabbing the remote, I pressed buttons until it shut up, then I froze. My heart was pounding. Was there someone in the house with me? My mind raced through thoughts of burglars and stalkers for a few moments, but there I heard nothing else.

Had something fallen over upstairs? If so, I was going to feel like a complete idiot, over-reacting like that. I snorted at myself and slid off the sofa, making as little noise as I could and avoiding the patch of water where I'd dropped my glass.

I crept into the kitchen and opened one of the drawers, pulling out the biggest knife I could see before heading for the stairs. There was no way I was going to investigate strange noises in an empty house without a weapon; I'd seen enough horror movies to know that. Up the stairs, with my knife held out in front of me, I peered up between the banisters and scanned the landing. There was nothing there; no feet, no shadows, nothing. I turned on the light, and nothing moved.

My ears were still straining, but my heart was slowing down now and I took a deep breath to calm myself even more. I checked the bathroom, mum's room, and then mine – there was nothing and no one there. I couldn't understand it.

After one last check, I went back downstairs, feeling silly with that big knife in my hands and hoping Mum wouldn't come home and find me like that. I put it back in the kitchen, grabbed a tea-towel and mopped up all the water I'd spilled on the sofa, wracking my brains for what could have caused all that noise.

Our house was small. There wasn't anywhere to hide, and we weren't terraced with anyone else's house, so we didn't get noises traveling through the walls from our neighbour's like some people. I just couldn't understand it. It had been so loud – as though something huge had smashed to pieces.

I looked at the clock; it was only half past five. Mum wouldn't be home for at least another hour yet. I sighed and rubbed my face. My head wasn't aching anymore. My doze on the sofa seemed to have helped. Maybe I should try and get on with some homework – it would give me more free time with Milly over the weekend. Telling myself I didn't have to do much, I got up and walked over to the stairs, grabbing my rucksack on the way.

Only a couple of steps from the top, another huge noise burst out around me, making me jump backwards into the wall. I dropped my school bag and it crashed down the stairs and into one of Mum's cabinets with another crack. My hands were shaking as I peered around the banisters onto the landing to see what had caused the noise. I couldn't see anything on the shadowy landing that could have caused that noise.

I breathed out and my lungs stung with the effort of

holding my breath. What was going on? Forcing my shaking legs to move, I crept up into the hallway and put the light back on, wincing at the thought of what I might see. But there was still nothing there.

I swore under my breath and took another step. There had to be someone in here with me; there was no other explanation. But should I try and find out where they were or should I just go downstairs and call the police? I could go next door – Mrs. Busher knew I was on my own – but then what would I tell Mum?

A horrible wave of nerves ran over me and I almost turned back to the stairs, then I forced myself to take another deep breath. If someone was in the house and wanted to hurt me, they'd already had their chance. They must have watched me look around before and I'd been pretty much asleep for almost an hour on the sofa. No, something else was going on here, and I was going to find out what.

Grabbing a heavy candlestick from a chest beside the bathroom door, I tiptoed along the landing, my eyes wide. There was no sound but my own breathing and the soft scuffling of my feet on the carpet, but I knew something was there. I could feel it.

I pushed Mum's bedroom door open as silently as I could, trying to figure out what was giving me the creeps. The light from the hallway illuminated enough of her room for me to be sure there was no one in there – it was so packed with shelves and trunks; there was hardly any room to stand, let alone hide. Taking a deep breath, I backed out into the corridor and turned to my right.

I was getting closer; the strange feeling was getting stronger as I crept across the landing to my bedroom door. There was nowhere else to hide. I took another breath and hesitated in front of the door. There was still time to go back downstairs and call the police, or just leave. I didn't have to go in there. But I wasn't going to make a fool of myself by calling a false alarm, or worry Mum by leaving the house and having to explain what had happened. What if it was just a cat that had slipped in somehow? No, I would check for myself.

Reaching out to the door, I felt the wood beneath my hand and frowned. It was freezing cold – so cold that my fingertips turned numb almost immediately. I shivered and pushed it open. The door swung back, throwing light from the hallway across the carpet and all the way to the opposite wall. I stood for a moment on the threshold, glaring into every nook and cranny of the room as my eyes adjusted to the shadows. But there was nothing there. Nothing had moved, nothing was broken, and there was certainly no one standing or hiding anywhere. There were no cupboards or wardrobes to climb into, and the window was shut and locked as usual. I frowned and stepped into the room, holding my candlestick high and feeling a little ridiculous again.

Nothing. I reached out and switched on the light. Still nothing. I stared around me, checking everything, even peering under the bed. Putting down the candlestick, I sat down at the desk and put my head in my hands. I must be going mental, I thought. There was nothing here that could have caused the noise, and I just couldn't figure it out. My heart was still pounding and I felt like I'd run a marathon, but there was no reason for any of it. No one was here.

I groaned and rubbed my face, forcing myself not to cry. The clock on my desk was showing half six.

"No way," I said, feeling even worse. I'd spent almost an hour creeping around in the dark. It was too late to do any homework now.

Getting up and grabbing the candlestick, I headed back onto the landing. I still felt creeped out – like someone was standing right behind me – but I told myself to just grow up. Slamming the candlestick back on its shelf, I turned off all the lights and huffed my way back downstairs to tidy up all the junk that had fallen out of my bag.

It was amazing how much stuff I'd collected over only half a week of school: broken pens, paper clips, bits of paper with scribbled notes, empty crisp packets and various hair clips were littering the floor along with most of my books and pens. I sighed and began to scoop it all back up, sifting through the rubbish so I could dump it in the bin where it belonged.

Then I paused; a gorgeous green and silver ring lay amongst the mess. I picked it up and turned it over in my hand. Where the hell had it come from and why was it in my bag? I'd never seen it before, and it looked valuable. In fact, it looked just like some of the antique jewelery Mum worked with, but that was impossible. I wondered if maybe it had been on the cabinet and fallen off when my bag hit it, but then I dismissed the idea. It was all mixed in with my things; it couldn't have gotten there unless it had been inside the bag itself. And anyway, why would a ring like this just be lying around our house?

The sound of a car starting up in the street reminded me what I was supposed to be doing. I had to get this cleaned away before Mum got home or she'd ask questions. I stuffed the ring into my pocket and carried on tidying up. I slung my bag into the corner when I'd finished, then headed for the living room.

I was feeling much better. Finding the ring and cleaning up my stuff had taken my mind off the total weirdness of the last few hours and how annoyed I'd been with myself. And luckily, by the time my mind started whirring over what had happened, Mum's car was pulling up outside. I dragged myself off the sofa and went to meet her at on the pavement.

"Hi, love," she said before turning to pull her bag out of the backseat.

"Hi," I said, surprised at how relieved I was that she was home. She hurried over and we stepped back into the house, then shut the door.

"God, I had such a day," she said.

"Yeah?" I asked.

"Another of those horrific meetings," she said, glancing at me. "Your father was there."

I caught her eye then looked away. "Oh."

"He sent his love," she said before hurrying to change the subject. I knew it was tricky for her, seeing him at work and having to pass on his messages. There was no way I was going to ask her about him.

"I had a bad day too," I said. I took some of her work folders from her.

"Oh?" She looked concerned. "Nothing that bad, I hope?"

I shrugged. "Emily and Holly aren't talking to me."

"What? Why?"

I shrugged again. "Who knows, I don't care anyway."

She gave me a look. "Really?"

I didn't have an answer for her.

She sighed. "I'm sorry, Annie. I've been really busy this week," she said, putting a hand on my shoulder for a moment. "And it was such an important week for you."

"It's okay," I said. "It's just school."

She gave me a sad smile then turned to pull out some pans for dinner. "Are you seeing Milly tomorrow?"

"Yeah," I said, "we're going to do our homework together."

I went to help her but she waved me away.

"No, sit down," she said, pushing me towards the table.

"You look exhausted."

I didn't argue with her. My head was starting to pound again and my stomach was growling. I remembered I'd hardly eaten when I got home and decided not to mention that.

"Sounds good," she said, glancing over her shoulder. "Doing your homework with Milly, I mean."

"Yeah, it'll be good. Hopefully we'll finish in time to do something fun together too."

The kitchen began to fill with delicious smelling steam and the sound of sizzling; Mum was a genius at cooking good meals in almost no time. My mouth began to water and I got myself a drink to hide how hungry I was. I was almost back to normal after my adventure of earlier, but not quite. I didn't want Mum noticing the slight shake in my hands and asking me questions.

"What have you been doing since you got home then?" she asked over her shoulder.

I shrugged and took a gulp of drink, spilling most of it down my top. Mum laughed. "Are you sure you're okay?" she said, throwing a tea towel at me so I could mop myself up.

I nodded and put down my glass. "I'm fine," I said. "Just a bit tired. I fell asleep on the sofa and didn't wake up for ages."

There was no need for me to go into exactly how long I'd slept, or anything that had happened after wards. I was in luck; her own bad day had obviously tired her out too, and she was too keen to get eating to look too closely at me. She grabbed some plates and began dishing our meal.

For a while, neither of us said anything. I didn't want to start talking and betray anything about my afternoon, so I just focused on eating. Mum was lost in through too, until finally I leaned back in my chair and let my cutlery clatter onto my plate.

I sighed. She grinned, wiping her mouth with a napkin and stretching in her seat.

"Thanks, Mum. That was great."

The food had filled me with a warm, relaxed feeling. I yawned. She winked at me.

"So what's in the cards for the rest of the evening? You've got another hour until bedtime. Do you want to watch a film with me?"

I shook my head, feeling my eyelids drooping already. "I'm so tired. I think I might just go and read in bed until I fall asleep."

"Probably for the best," she said, shaking her head at me. "I've never seen you so tired before."

"I can't believe how hard school is." I stifled a yawn. "I don't know if I'll ever get used to it."

She smiled and squeezed my hand. "Don't worry about it. Everyone feels like that at first – just ask Milly."

"I know. That's exactly what she said. But I doubt she was this tired at first!"

Mum shook her head and got up to do the washing up.

"Do you want any help?" I asked.

She shook her head and flicked on the radio. "No," she said over her shoulder. "Just go and rest, my love. Thank you." She waved me out of the kitchen. She was singing along to the radio the moment my feet touched the stairs.

I hadn't told her anything about my week, but I felt better. Just knowing she'd be here for most of the weekend and we'd have a whole evening together tomorrow made going to bed early okay. My eyes were aching and my head was stuffed with cotton wool. I pushed open my bedroom door and flicked on the light.

SEVEN

My whole body froze mid-stride. Standing right in the middle of the floor was a dark figure. Not a person, but a shape; featureless, silent, still. A shadow without a source.

It seemed like years passed before I could blink. Then the figure was gone. I stood staring at the spot where it had been, my mouth hanging open as I gripped the doorknob to keep myself upright. What the hell had that been? I shook my head and blinked again. Nothing moved; there was no dark figure on the carpet. My room looked normal.

I edged my way through the door and looked around. Everything was as I'd left it; nothing had been touched. There was nowhere for a person to hide or escape, no lamp or statue to throw a shadow like that in the middle of the air. I couldn't understand it.

For a moment, I thought about calling for Mum and telling her what I'd seen, but I dismissed the idea as soon as I thought it. There was no way I was going to worry her; it would inevitably lead to me telling her about this afternoon, and she already felt guilty enough about me having to be home alone. No, I was just tired – that was all. I'd been all worked up over the mysterious sounds earlier, got myself really messed up about it and not been able to think it through yet. Add that to how tired I was and my row with Emily, and it was no wonder I was falling for tricks of the light.

I nodded to myself and tried to swallow that same crawling pressure in my throat. There was nothing to worry about. I was not going mad, and there was no one in my room. I told myself to get over it one more time then got ready for bed, forcing myself to slowly go through each step so that the lurking panic in my stomach wouldn't rise and take over.

After twenty minutes, I was climbing into my warm bed with a good book. Mum had brought me a cup of tea and left it on the bedside table. I concentrated on drinking it and the shivering, creepy feeling faded. I felt way better than I had all evening. Sleep was lulling my mind, warm and soft, and I snuggled into my pillow to read for a while before it overtook me completely.

৪৩৫৪

I was running faster than I ever had before. Branches stung my face and hands as I pushed past them, their needles snagging my clothes. Blood pounded in my ears like a thunder, driving me forward. I sucked at the cold air through dry lips, panting and forcing myself to keep running. Something was behind me. Something cold, something big. Up ahead, tiny snowflakes began to fall, spiraling through the air between the trees and dancing as I sped past. My feet thudded on the frozen ground, but I was fast; I was almost flying.

The trees opened and the ground fell away. I was gone; I

was free, soaring away.

The dream changed. I stood in the hallway of my house. Everything was dark and still. Something I'd forgotten nagged at the back of my mind, but I brushed it away; I was glad to be home.

In a moment, I was moving upwards, around the staircase to the upper floor. Nothing moved. My mother was in bed; I could feel her slow, small breathing from behind the bedroom door like a creature stirring just out of sight. I turned and looked towards my own bedroom. The door got bigger, looming above me – darker and larger than I remembered it. Putting out my hand, I noticed icicles clinging to the door frame like dull glass, and I felt the cold air pouring out from under the wood.

The door swung open. The room beyond was dark; at first I could see nothing. Moving closer, the features of the room solidified around me. Something was moving ahead of me; I could hear the slow breathing of someone sleeping, warm and still on the bed. And above the sleeping figure, something hung in the air, frozen like a photograph.

My breath billowed grey in front of my face, fading the edges of the room. Cold seared my bare feet and the skin of my hands and face; I could feel it sliding beneath my clothes like hands, numbing my flesh. I tried to speak, to move, but I was frozen solid and horror clung in my throat like vomit. I watched the shape above the sleeping body, as slowly –so slowly –it moved, dipping closer to the bed. It seemed to me like hands of smoke were reaching out from the vague form, solidifying above the motionless body.

My heart was going to burst, just shatter into a million frozen pieces. I wanted to scream at it, to force it away, but my body wouldn't listen to me. The room swam, clouds of breath swirled like mist, and then the ground lurched beneath my feet.

I fell, and then I landed, warm and panting, on something soft.

I gripped the mattress, pushed myself upright and opened my eyes. My chest ached like my ribs might break and I gasped as though I'd not breathed in minutes. Reaching up to my face, I felt my skin. It was warm and soft. A wave of hot relief flooded through me. It had been a dream. Just a crazy dream.

The house was quiet and the streetlights outside threw wide, reassuringly normal shadows across the floor. There were still cars driving in the distance; I couldn't have been asleep for long. Flopping back onto the bed, I pulled the bedclothes up to my chin and closed my eyes. Then I rolled over, turning my back to the room and letting let myself slide back into sleep.

EIGHT

I woke up to bright sunlight. Checking my clock, I was shocked to see it was already 9 – I never slept that late. I could hear Mum downstairs, clattering in the kitchen with the radio on low, and I felt more relaxed than I had in days. The bed was warm and comfy, and for a few minutes I was tempted to just turn over and go back to sleep.

Deciding I had too much to do to give into the temptation of a longer lie in, I slid out of bed and grabbed my dressing gown. My stomach was already rumbling and breakfast was absolutely necessary before I got dressed and called Milly.

"Good morning!" Mum came out of the kitchen and stood watching me come downstairs with a grin on her face. "I was beginning to wonder if you'd turned into one of those teenager creatures."

She stepped aside so I could get into the kitchen. The whole place was sparkling and there was a huge jug standing beside a heating frying pan.

"Pancakes!" I said, glancing at her.

She shrugged. "Just a little treat." She started pouring the first one into the pan. "To make up for my many absences this week."

I came up behind her and gave her a hug; she smelt of kitchen cleaner and fresh bread – an oddly nice combination.

"Thanks," I said, my mouth watering. The smell of cooking pancake filled the room and my stomach growled even louder.

I got myself a plate and some syrup, and Mum served up the pancakes as they cooked, hot and gooey. After a good 20 minutes, I felt a whole lot better than I had all week and sat back in my chair with a contented sigh.

"That was great." I yawned, stretching and running a hand through my bed hair. She put the jug of leftover batter back in the fridge, then walked over to the sink and turned on the tap over the dishes. "What time are you going 'round to Milly's?"

"I don't know," I said. "I need to call her."

She nodded, turning up the radio for one of her favourite songs. I decided I'd better have a shower and get dressed; it was beginning to feel weird to still be in my dressing gown. Then I remembered something.

"Hey, Mum," I said, getting to my feet.

"Mmm?"

"Hang on. I've got something to show you."

I hopped out of the room. Upstairs in my bedroom, I searched through my clothes until I found the mysterious ring that had appeared in my things last night, then I headed back downstairs.

"Do you know where this came from?" I said, holding it out. She put down a plate, still humming along to the music, and reached out for what I was holding. I tipped the ring into her palm and waited for her to answer. Holding it up to her face in practiced fingers, she gazed at it for a moment.

"Where did you get this?" she asked, not looking up. But her voice had changed just a little, and it was definitely closer to her telling-me-off voice than normal. I felt a sinking feeling in the bottom of my stomach.

"I found it – in my bag, with my things. I think it must have fallen in there."

She nodded, staring at the ring as she turned it over and over. Then she looked up and handed it back to me. I stared at her, taking the ring and waiting for her to speak.

"Well, I have no idea where it's come from," she said, giving me a piercing look. "It's certainly valuable, and old."

She kept on looking at me. My neck prickled like static and I shifted my weight.

"Are you sure you have no idea how it got in your bag?" she asked, her hands coming to rest on her hips.

I hesitated for a moment, but there was no reason to tell her about the strange noises yesterday. Surely, they had nothing to do with this ring. I shook my head.

"No," I said through a dry mouth.

She nodded once. "Okay. But if there's anything I need to know, now's the time to tell me."

I stared at her. The ring was cold and heavy in my fist, and my stomach felt like lead. "I don't know what you mean," I said, stuttering a little; Mum had never spoken to me like this.

"I think you do," she said, looking me in the eye. "If you say you don't know how you got it, then I believe you, but if I find out you're lying..."

"Lying about what? I don't understand what you're talking about."

"Okay," she said, nodding a little. "Okay then. That's fine – you'd better give it back to me and I'll take care of it until someone wants to claim it."

She held out her hand. For a moment, I thought about refusing, but what would be the point – I didn't care about the ring, just about whether or not she really thought I could have stolen it. I reached out and dropped it into her outstretched palm and she curled her fingers around it, then tucked it into her pocket.

We looked at each other for a moment. My cheeks felt hot, and I couldn't decide whether I was more hurt or angry; Mum had never talked to me like that and I hated it. It wasn't my fault the ring had gotten into my bag, but part of me understood why she was suspicious. It was a lame story.

I took a deep breath and tried to act normal; there was no point in getting into a big fight over it.

"I'm going to go and have a shower," I said.

Mum nodded; she was obviously trying to act normal too. "Okay," she said, turning back to the washing up. I watched her for a moment then turned and headed upstairs, my face burning.

I thought the whole thing over in the shower until the water ran cold. I couldn't explain about the ring any better than I already had, and trying to would just make things worse. Better to leave it, get on with my day and hope she'd forget about it later. I ducked into my room and grabbed the phone, then sat with my hair dripping on the bedspread as I dialed.

I was so glad I'd already made plans with Milly. Cheerful and wide awake, she pulled me out of my worries and told me to come straight 'round to her flat. It took me ten minutes to throw my things together and get out the door, and before I knew it Toady was letting me in with a grunt and waving at Milly's bedroom door. She was already hard at work on her cramped desk when I walked into the tiny, tidy room and dropped my bag on the carpet. She looked up from her work.

"You got up late," she said.

"Yeah." I stretched my shoulders out. That bag hadn't got

any lighter overnight. "I was exhausted last night. I had a really crazy dream, too."

She looked up again, her pen pausing in mid-air. "Oh yeah? What about?"

I shrugged. "I can't remember now," I told her, sitting on the edge of her bed. "But it was nuts. I didn't get much homework done either."

"Don't worry about it; I can help," she said, pulling some of her books off the bed so I could spread out.

We worked in silence for what felt like hours. My headache from the night before was threatening to come back – a dull thud grew at the edge of my brain until it felt like everything in there had turned to soup. I checked the clock; it was only half eleven. I groaned.

Milly glanced at me, then the clock and rolled her eyes. "I know." She stretched her arms above her head. "How much have you got left?"

"Loads," I moaned. "I can't believe how much homework they gave us on our first week!"

She nodded then closed her book. "I need something to eat," she said. "Shall we take a break?"

I dropped my pen with relief. There was no way I'd be good for more work any time soon.

"Let's have some lunch then maybe we can do something else?" I said.

Milly grinned. "My thoughts exactly." She scooped all her books into a pile and stood up. "Come on, let's make some lunch."

My aunt was sitting at the living room table with the thick shop ledgers spread in front of her when we emerged.

"How's it going?" she asked.

"Great," Milly called, already through the arch that separated the kitchen from the living room. "We're starving now though."

"Okay," I added, stopping next to the Sandy and rubbing my aching head.

Sandy squeezed my arm. "Milly said you're having trouble. It'll get easier," she told me. "Milly does fine, and look how much school she misses!"

I rolled my eyes. "That's 'cause she's Milly, and she's awesome," I said, and Sandy laughed. In the kitchen, I could already hear Milly clattering plates and cutlery out of cupboards and onto the sideboard. "I'd better go and help."

"Make sure you two have some fun this afternoon, okay?"

I waved at her and joined Milly in the cramped kitchen just as she closed the fridge door and picked up our plates. "Glad your mum's feeling better," I said.

"Yeah, me too." Milly handed me a plate holding a chunky sandwich with cheese spilling out of it and a handful of salad leaves. Then she shrugged. "Sorry, I know it's not fancy but I'm too hungry to wait."

"I don't care," I told her. My stomach was growling embarrassingly at the sight of it. "Thanks for making it."

We hurried back to her room, closed the door and curled up crossed legged on Milly's bed, plates in front of us. Milly turned on some music.

"Thanks," I said again, tucking in.

Milly grinned at me, took a big bite of sandwich and turned the volume up. Then she gulped down some water and gave me a look. "Okay," she said, leaning forward. "I've been waiting all morning for this – spill."

I frowned at her, wondering what she was talking about.

"Oh come on," she went on, rolling her eyes. "I know something's up – and it's not just school stuff. So what it is?"

I put down my sandwich then looked at her. It was tempting

to shrug it off, but she was right. She'd know if I didn't tell her the truth, and I'd already lost too many friends this week. I sighed.

"Oh God," I said, rubbing my forehead. I tried to come up with a simple answer. "Where to start?"

Milly settled herself, lifted her sandwich again and said, "Start with last night."

So I did. I told her everything, even though I was convinced she'd either laugh at me or call my Mum to tell her I was nuts. I told her about the weird noises, and how scared I'd gotten, and the ring just turning up out of nowhere. I told her about having that stupid argument with Emily and how badly school had gone since then. And then I told her about the shadow I'd seen in my bedroom last night. By the time I finished, I was feeling kind of sick. My sandwich lay on my plate, untouched.

Milly leaned forward and hugged me. She hadn't laughed once. "I knew something weird was going on with you," she said. "What do you think it all means?"

I shrugged; I had no clue, not even a guess, as to what was going on.

"I have a confession," Milly went on, and I raised my eyebrows.

"Oh yeah?"

"Yeah. I saw something too, yesterday. In the shop."

I remembered the look on her face as I was leaving yesterday afternoon and felt a sinking feeling in my stomach. "What did you see?"

"It sounds just like what you described. A weird shadow. It vanished the moment I saw it. But it's odd, isn't it, that we've both seen it?"

"Around me," I added. "We've both see it around me."

I couldn't even begin to understand what that meant. I

scrunched my eyes up against the stinging in them. It had been a bad week.

Milly hugged me again, tighter and longer. "Don't worry about it," she said. "You've had a big week, a lot going on, and it's normal to feel a bit off, okay?"

I nodded.

"Seriously," she went on, "don't worry about it. Here, eat your lunch – I made it especially for you."

She made a funny face and I couldn't help laughing. I took the plate from her and took another bite of sandwich while Milly filled me in on her own week with as much humour as she could. By the time I finished, I almost felt like a normal person again.

NINE

"Well?" Milly stacked our plates on the side then turned back to me with her hands on her hips. "What do you want to do now?"

I was leaning against the kitchen wall, enjoying the sunshine on my face. I shrugged; I didn't want to choose for her, but I'd love to get out into that bright weather.

Milly smiled. "Do you fancy going out on the bikes for a bit?"

I grinned and nodded. "That'd be great."

She grinned back and waved for me to follow her out the kitchen door, down the side stairs and out into the alley behind the shop. This was where she, Toady and I kept our bikes locked in a rickety, metal shed. She unlocked the door and wheeled hers out first, then reached right to the back for mine. She frowned.

"What's the matter?" I asked, holding her bike for her and leaning closer to see what she was looking at. She shook her head and said nothing until she dragged my bike out into the light where I could immediately see what the problem was. Both tired had been shredded; the rubber was hanging from the frames in tatters. They were useless.

"I'm so sorry," she said, looking up at me. "I have no idea how this happened."

A horrible thought entered my mind, and before I could stop it the words were out of my mouth. "Are you sure it wasn't Toady?"

I clapped my hand to my mouth, horrified at what I'd said, but Milly just shook her head. "It can't have been," she said. "He went out just after you got here and when I looked in the bike shed earlier, your bike was fine."

I leaned back against the grubby brick wall and my heart sank; this was just what I needed.

"I'm really sorry," she said again.

I stepped closer to her, maneuvering the bikes out of the way so I could give her an awkward hug. "Hey," I said, "it's not your fault."

She blinked and wiped her eyes. "Are you sure you're not mad? I have no idea how it happened."

I squeezed her. "Of course I'm not mad – it's not like you did it," I told her with a smile. She smiled back. I crouched down and looked closer at the wheels. "You know," I said, "it actually looks like an animal did this – maybe a rat. It's not like it's been cut with a knife."

Milly shook her head. "This is so weird," she said, wheeling the bikes back into the shed. "Why would a rat chew up just the one bike?"

"I have no idea," I said, laughing a little at how crazy it was. "But to be honest, with all the other strange stuff that's been happening lately, I'm not that surprised."

Milly raised an eyebrow and bent over the shed padlock. It closed with a click and she gave it a tug.

"Maybe we should just go back upstairs and finish our

homework," I said, kicking at the wall with my heel.

Milly shook her head. "No way." A defiant grin spread across her face. "This weather's too good to miss and it won't last much longer." She pulled me out of the alley, looking suddenly excited. "Let's walk to the woods - take a picnic for dinner so we can stay as long as we want."

It was the best thing I'd heard all day. But I hesitated, just for a moment.

"You do want to, don't you?" she asked.

"I do," I told her. "It's just…is it okay to leave your mum for that long?"

She swatted the worry away. "It's fine," she said. "She's fine now – you saw. We'll let her know where we're going and be back before it gets dark. Toady'll be home in the next hour or so anyway."

I returned her grin and followed her back up to the flat. The woods that ran along our side of town were our favourite place in the world; we'd been going there together as long as I could remember. It would be great to get back there; it had been a few weeks since Milly had been able to go out that long. Normally, we only stayed for an hour, and I was always sad to leave. It would be a proper adventure, eating our dinner there by ourselves, maybe even exploring further than we ever had before.

We hurried upstairs and began to get our picnic ready. Milly ran into the living room to ask her mum what we could take from the kitchen, and I could hear them talking about our plan as I emptied my schoolbag, ready to fill it with treats.

Then Milly ran back into the kitchen, grinning from ear to ear. "She says we can have whatever we want," she told me, almost hopping from foot to foot.

"That's great," I said, looking around the kitchen. "What is there?"

"She means from the shop, too," Milly explained, and I realised why she was so excited. My aunt owned a deli; it was full of snacks and delicious treats that we weren't usually allowed to take. We hurried down the back stairs and into the shop.

"She must be in a good mood," I said.

"She's pleased we're going out."

The shop was so pretty in the bright sunshine that streamed through the wide windows, full of colourful exotic fruits, handmade snacks and the delicious smell of spices. We took a moment to appreciate all that treasure, waved at Carrie on the till and began stuffing our bags with all of our favourites.

Neither of us stopped until both rucksacks were full to the brim. They would be pretty heavy to carry out there, but we had lots of time and it would be worth it for the feast we'd have in the shade of the trees. Milly ran to the bottom of the stairs and called up to her mum that we were off, then we headed out the front doors, waving on our way past the counter. Carrie laughed as we passed her, but we didn't care. We had all afternoon, and I'd forgotten about my horrible week.

"I guess we do look pretty silly," I said, "getting this excited about a trip to the woods."

Milly shrugged. "Hey," she said, "I don't get to go out much and it's my favourite place."

"Me too."

We reached the end of the road and slowed down. It was too hot in the sun to hurry and our bags were heavy. We walked for about an hour, talking a bit but mostly just taking in the quiet afternoon. It wasn't often we came this way –we always took the roads when we cycled – but seeing as we were taking our time and had all afternoon before we had to be back, we wandered along the river bank that ran opposite the line of big houses and big gardens marking the edge town.

The weather was perfect. We spent most of the walk spotting dragon flies and swans out on the slow-moving water, and hearing the scurrying of voles in the undergrowth. Slowing down was everything I needed. I could just feel myself catching my breath as the weight of my week lifted.

It was nearly two by the time we turned off the road and onto the first path into the woods. The grass on either side was high. It smelt fresh and damp after last night's rain, and the birches lining the walk rustled in the breeze. We both took a deep breath and I felt the last of my tension leave me as the dappled shadows passed over my face.

Milly and I looked at each other and grinned; this was more like it. Being anywhere but here on a day like today would have been a waste. I was so glad we'd decided to come that even my bike's slashed tires couldn't bother me. We would only have come for an hour or so with the bikes. This was much, much better.

The noises of the town faded behind us and we met no one else on the path except a few sleepy bees. We meandered through the lighter parts of the woods for a while, heading in the direction of our favourite spot. It was a shady knoll, overlooking a small stream that ran quick and clear towards the larger river. It was a hard place to get to, nestled between tall thickets of brambles on one side and the stream's wild banks on the other.

We threw down our packs with a sigh, rubbing our shoulders and wiping the sweat from our foreheads. The hottest time of the day had passed while we were walking and that last climb up to the knoll was hard going through all the bushes. I was dead thirsty, and looking forward to taking off my shoes and dangling my feet in the cool water.

"Here," Milly said, handing me an open bottle of ginger beer.

I took a swig. "This is perfect," I said, handing it back and looking around us. No sounds but the trees and the stream could be heard this far from town. I threw myself down beside her and kicked off my shoes.

"Ahhh," Milly sighed, lying down with her eyes closed and stretching out in the sunlight. I grinned at her and shuffled over to the bank to dip my feet into the stream. Neither of us moved or spoke for a long time.

But, slowly, I realised this visit wasn't like the others. The whole place felt different; I couldn't put my finger on it, but something had changed. While I lay with my feet in the freezing water wondering what it was, Milly sat up behind me and rummaged in her bag.

"What are you looking for?" I asked over my shoulder. She flashed me a smile and kept searching. I pulled my feet out of the stream and crawled over to sit beside her. Finally, she pulled a thick red-bound book out of the bottom of her rucksack and sat back, looking satisfied.

"I knew I hadn't forgotten it," she said, stroking the cover. "It was just under all the food."

"What is it?" I asked, reaching out to take it from her. She moved away a little – just a small movement, but enough to tell me not to touch the book. I looked at her with more amazement. She blushed.

"It's a book I've wanted to look at for ages," she said, looking down at it with wide eyes, "but I can never get the time at home."

"You read all the time at home," I said, perplexed.

Milly stared at me for a few moments, chewing her lip.

"Yeah," she said eventually. "But I don't read anything like this at home. Mum would have a fit if she saw it."

Now I was curious; what book could possibly get my aunt that upset? She was normally so laid back about everything. I leaned closer, trying to get a look at the gold lettering on the front.

"Okay," I said. "So, what is it? What's it about?"

I could feel my neck prickling under my hair, and I wondered if I really wanted to know the answer to my question. What if it was something bad, or embarrassing? I didn't think Milly would look at anything like that, but I couldn't think of anything else she'd have to hide.

Milly looked down at the book for a moment before answering; she seemed to be running something through in her mind. "It was Grandma's," she said. I waited for her to continue, knowing this would be interesting – our Grandma was a bit of a sore point for the whole family. Milly took another deep breath before she went on.

"She left it to me in her will," she said. "Mum wasn't pleased, but she let it slide. She hid it though, in the attic, and I haven't seen it in years. But then I found it a couple of weeks ago and I've been waiting for a chance to look at it properly ever since." She stared up at me, holding my gaze. "And I wanted to share it with you, too," she said, swallowing. "I think you'll find it interesting."

I shook my head. "I still don't understand."

She leaned in a little, lowering her voice and looking around as though she thought someone could be watching us.

"I mean, with your... little problem," she said, giving me a meaningful look.

I stared at her, nonplussed.

She sighed then rolled her eyes. "You know, that shadow-thing."

She said it as though it was obvious. But I shook my head at her. "Why would Grandma's book have anything to do with that?" I asked.

Milly hesitated, shifting on the blanket. "You mean you don't know?"

"Know what?" I asked, starting to get annoyed.

"Grandma," she whispered with bright eyes, "was a witch."

TEN

I stared at Milly, trying to figure out if she was having me on. This had to be a joke. But Milly never played jokes on me; that just wasn't the kind of friendship we had.

But if it wasn't a joke, I couldn't understand why she was saying this. It was crazy. Grandma was a normal, old lady I had only met once. She'd fallen out with her children, Aunt Sandy and my dad, over something adult and boring. Okay, she was a bit odd, from what people said about her, but she had certainly not been a witch!

I almost laughed, not knowing what else to do. But Milly was looking at me steadily, not even a hint of a smile. She was still holding that little red book in her lap and waiting for me to say something.

"I'm sorry," I said. "I still don't understand."

There was a pause.

"Okay," she said, laying the book next to her and leaning back on her elbows. "I know this sounds a bit weird –really weird, actually –but it's definitely true."

"But I still don't know what you mean."

Milly held up her hand for me to wait, then said, "Hang on

then; I'll explain."

I shut up and waited for her to continue, impatient.

"Grandma Orr was a witch. A real, actual witch – not like in movies and books. This little book," she pointed at the book lying beside her, "was her journal, and she left it to me before she died, with a letter explaining all about it."

Milly paused, and I stared at her, not knowing what to say.

"My mum and your dad," she continued, "they both know about it, but they pretend not to," she continued. "I don't know why – maybe they're embarrassed or afraid or something, but they had a big falling out over it when I was born because Grandma wanted to tell me about it and they didn't want her to. It was the same with you too."

"The same how?" I asked.

"Grandma wanted to teach you too, but your dad wouldn't have it so they argued and Grandma was kind of shut out," she said, sighing a little.

"Why don't I know any of this?" I asked, still unsure if I believed any of it.

"Well obviously, they didn't tell us – we were really little. All they told us was they fell out over something or other, and that Grandma was a weird old lady who we weren't allowed to talk to."

I nodded; this much was familiar. "So, how come you found out?"

"Her letter explained all of it," Milly said. "That's the first time I heard about it."

"So you've known for years," I said, and she nodded.

"Yes, but I had no proof. Mum took the book and destroyed the letter."

I gaped at her; I couldn't imagine Aunt Sandy doing something like that.

Milly nodded again. "I know," she said, "but she really, really hates this stuff – it's the only thing I just can't talk about with her."

"Still," I said, "I can't believe she would do that. Grandma was her own mother."

Milly shrugged. "They hadn't spoken in years by the time Grandma died," she said, "and Mum was still furious."

We sat in silence for a minute. It appeared to me that families were really complicated, and I'd hate to fall out like that with my mum. I looked up as Milly continued.

"So it's true. She was a witch, and our parents – well my mum and your dad at least – knew it."

"And," I said, "if what you're saying is true, she thought we could be too."

Milly nodded. "Exactly. Now can you see why I was so excited when I found the book? Why I wanted to bring it with me today?"

"Yeah," I said, grinning. "Definitely. But what I still don't understand is, well, what do you mean by 'witch'?"

"Good question," Milly said, nodding. "I wondered the same thing when I read the letter. I mean, the only things I knew about witches back then was they were covered in warts, wore black and rode broomsticks!" She laughed.

"That's all I know about them now," I said with a frown. How could I have missed out on such big part of my family's history? I felt like an idiot.

"That's not your fault," she said, and I could tell she knew what I was feeling. "I mean, why would you know any more? That's all we see in books and films and stuff, and it's not like you've had any reason to investigate more."

That made me feel a little better about being so out of the loop.

"Okay," I said. "So, what do you know about witches now?"

Milly grinned widely, her eyes sparkling the way they always did when she was really excited. "Well," she said, settling herself lower on the blanket. "I've managed to do some research on my own. It's not like I could ask Mum or anything, but I've looked stuff up in the library, in books and on the internet. Now there's a lot of rubbish." She rolled her eyes at the thought of it. "But I've found a couple of bits and pieces that seem a bit more like it; they fit more with what Grandma said in her letter anyway."

"What did she say?"

"I can't remember the exact words – I mean, I only saw it once about 6 years ago! But she said that 'witch' was the closest word in English to what she meant, and it was all about the seasons, and being in tune with nature and... and, oh, loads of stuff. It was a long letter."

"I can't believe you managed to read it even once," I said, shaking my head.

"I know, I was so lucky. Mum just didn't see it when it arrived, and by the time I'd told her about it, I'd already read it properly."

"Lucky," I agreed.

There was another moment of silence before I continued; this was a lot to take in. "So, my next questions is, what is a witch? And what's in that book?"

I pointed to where Grandma's journal lay beside her, like a bomb waiting to be triggered. Milly glanced at it too, then grinned.

"I have no idea what's in the book," she said, "but I'm hoping it'll give us more information on what she was doing and what she wanted to teach us than what I've found so far."

I nodded, waiting for her to answer my first question.

"As for what a witch is – I still have no idea. I don't know if anyone does! There seems to be so many answers to that. But there seem to be themes, things everyone agrees on, and they do make sense with what I know about Grandma."

"Go on," I said.

"Well, it is a lot about nature, and being with nature, and working with nature," Milly said, looking around us at the woods and stream.

"There's lots of these ceremonies and rituals that match the seasons, stuff like that," she continued, "as well as other stuff – stuff I don't understand at all. That's what's I'm hoping Grandma will have written about."

"What stuff?" I asked.

She leaned in to me a little, lowering her voice again. "Working with Spirits and Goddesses and things like that," she said, her voice full of tightly controlled energy. "And spells for protection and healing."

I sat back a little, saying nothing. This was all completely crazy. Milly must have gotten it wrong. Maybe she really was playing a joke on me. There was no way me or my family could have anything to do with this. We were so normal! And yet, somewhere inside me it felt right. I couldn't explain it; I wouldn't even be able to describe it in words, but what she was saying about working with nature and even the stuff about spirits and rituals felt familiar and true. It was like something I'd known a long time ago and had just forgotten for a while.

I looked up and realised Milly was watching me. Her face was a little pale. "Are you okay?" she asked.

I hesitated, then nodded. "Are you okay?" I asked, looking closely at her.

"Yeah," she said, letting out a long, slow breath. "Sorry. It's just, well, I've been wanting to tell you all this for ages – for years, actually – and now it's come and I'm a bit nervous about how you'll react."

I flopped down on the ground beside her and sighed. "Don't be silly," I told her.

We grinned at each other then I looked up at the sky above us. I was more aware of the trees, the grasses and the stream than I had ever been before; it all felt real and close, with the two of us together at the centre. It was an odd feeling, but a nice one.

"So," I said, turning to catch Milly's eye again. "Let's look at that book."

It was like I'd been struck by lightning; I felt like my whole body was vibrating and tingling and more alive than ever before. The journal lay on the rough grass between us, and Milly's face shone with excitement as she reached down for it. She lifted it into her lap, and I got to really look at it for the first time.

It was small and innocent-looking, worn and faded but obviously well cared for, with a cover of soft, red leather. It occurred to me the journal was probably over 80 years old, maybe even 100. I was amazed we were looking at it at all; the odds against it reaching us were so huge.

Milly looked down at the book too, running her fingers over the binding as though she wanted to memorise every bump. I understood what she was feeling. This was an amazing moment; it felt like destiny in a way I would never be able to explain to anyone else.

"Okay," Milly took a deep breath and reached for the clasp at the edge of the book. "Ready?"

I nodded. I couldn't say anything; my heart was pounding so hard in my throat.

She took the little clasp in her fingers and flicked it open, then lifted the front cover and laid the book out flat in her lap so we could both see it. The inner leaf was covered in a rainbow of beautiful, inked spirals and the first page had the initials C. A. O. written in pencil on the yellowing paper.

"Well," I said, tracing the initials with a finger tip. "It's definitely hers."

Milly laughed. "A right fool I'd feel if I'd made all this fuss over some random old book!"

I laughed with her, feeling the tension pour out of me. It was just a book. Nothing scary had happened. We giggled and looked back down at the journal. But the moment Milly rested her fingers against the edge of the pages, my head filled with questions and I felt the tension return. What would we find in this book? Would it explain any of the weird stuff that had happened this week? Was this really a good idea?

The bushes right behind me shivered a little. Then they shivered again, this time more violently, tossing leaves to the ground and filling the clearing with the sound of ripping, cracking undergrowth. We both jumped and I turned around so fast that my neck jarred. But there was nothing there; the movement had stopped as suddenly as it had started.

I turned back and met Milly's wide eyes. "Do you think there's someone there?" she whispered.

"I don't know."

I glanced over my shoulder again and felt a chill run through me. At least an hour had passed since we'd arrived; the sun was lower in the sky, just dipping to touch the line of treetops, and the shadows had grown long and cool. No one usually came to this part of the wood, not even dog walkers. What if someone had followed us?

Milly was braver than me. Grabbing the book and standing up, she peered into the bushes. "Is someone there?" she asked, stepping closer to the edge of the woods.

My stomach writhed and tied itself in knots, but nothing

happened. No voice called back; nothing moved.

Milly stood staring for a few more moments, then lowered herself back down and shrugged. "It must have been an animal," she said. "Foxes come out at dusk."

Her voice was loud and awkward in the quiet now. I swallowed. If it hadn't been for all the strange things I'd seen and heard in the last few days, I would have had no problem believing her explanation, but now I was finding it hard to brush off what had just happened. I felt cold and shivery and a little bit sick.

Milly took one look at me and shook her head. "You need some food," she said, reaching for our bags and pulling them closer. "Here."

She handed me the feast; bags of nuts and seeds and dried fruit together with pots of dips and bags of crisps. I began pulling them all open and setting them out; my stomach was tight and sore from the tension, and I realised I was starving. We tucked in, and for a little while there no sounds except for the crinkle of paper bags and the gentle chiming of the stream.

The food definitely helped me feel better. My cheeks got warm again and my hands stopped shaking, and eventually the tight feeling inside me began to unwind. Milly watched me as we ate, but it didn't bother me; I knew she was just being my friend. I would have done the same for her.

Once we'd eaten all we wanted and packed away the leftovers, Milly grinned and pulled out a large metal canteen from the bottom of her bag.

"When did you make that?" I asked.

She unscrewed the top and poured out two large mugs of hot chocolate. Milly winked at me and handed me a cup. I breathed in the sweet steam and sighed.

"When you were unpacking your bag," she said, taking a

careful sip and then giving a deep sigh of satisfaction. "Ah, that's better."

I sipped too, feeling the warmth spreading through my body from my stomach. It was just what I needed.

"Thank you," I said. "This is perfect."

"Feeling better?"

I nodded.

"Thought so," she said. "This'll help you warm up."

I nodded, then said, "I've been really hungry lately. And tired. I think it's all this work my brain's doing after a summer of being stupid."

Milly laughed. "Maybe."

We drank in silence for a while. The eerie feeling had faded; now the woods felt still and peaceful as the warmth of the afternoon turned into the gold-pink light of dusk. It was beautiful.

"We should start heading back," Milly said, finishing her hot chocolate. She got up to rinse the cups in the stream.

"I suppose." I felt so at home there. I was relaxed for the first time that week.

She glanced at me over her shoulder. "It's going to take us ages to get home," she said.

"I know. It's just so lovely here," I said, then added, "and we didn't get to read any of the book."

Milly sighed and began packing up her bag.

"Well," she said, "we'll just have to create another opportunity to look at it, won't we?"

We smiled at each other; now this mystery was in front of me there was no way I was going to just walk away. I wanted to know more. I swung my bag onto my back and followed Milly as she began to pick our path out through the trees.

"You know, you could come 'round to my house and we

could look at it there," I suggested.

"That would work, if we did it when your mum wasn't there," she said over her shoulder.

We slipped back into silence as we navigated the tangle of bushes and trees, but I kept thinking about how we could get some time alone with Grandma's book. The more I thought about it, the more important it felt.

By the time we reached the road, I was almost bursting with impatience. Milly took one look at me and laughed. "Oh God," she said. "I'm sorry. Maybe I shouldn't have told you!"

"No way!" I said. "I'm so glad you did; it's really exciting. Though I don't know why."

Milly slowed down to walk beside me.

"It just feels..." I tried to find the right words. "It feels right. Important somehow. Do you know what I mean?"

Milly nodded. "I know exactly what you mean," she said. Then she sighed. "That's how I've felt ever since I found out about it. That's why I didn't just give up."

I gave her a squeeze. "I'm glad you didn't."

After a few steps, I went back to the subject that was foremost in my mind. "You know," I said, "we could meet up tomorrow at my house. Mum's out all day."

But Milly sighed and shook her head. "No, I'm going with Mum to see Uncle Mike and the baby; we'll be there all day. Sorry."

"That's okay," I said, my heart sinking. We probably wouldn't get any time during the week, which meant it might be next weekend before we'd get another opportunity.

Milly reached around my shoulders and squeezed me. "Don't worry. One thing I've learnt from all of this so far is that the book wants us to read it. I can't explain how it survived otherwise."

I nodded, not really understanding what she meant. But I trusted Milly, and I knew she wouldn't let this go now she'd told me. She was the most determined person I knew. "Okay."

"Come on," she said. "Your Mum'll worry if we're too late."

I watched her speed up and let her pull ahead of me. I suddenly felt tired again. It had been such a long week with so much to think about, and all I wanted to do now was go home and curl up in bed. I sped up to catch up with her and we walked back towards town in silence. The sun was half beneath the horizon by the time we got to the shop. Milly hurried off with a quick hug and a wave, leaving me to walk the last few minutes on my own. My feet were dragging and my rucksack pulled my shoulders even though it was nearly empty; it was a huge effort to keep walking.

Mum was waiting for me in the open front door, which was a beacon of light in the grey, empty street. I hurried to meet her.

"Hi."

"Hi there." She stepped back to let me in. "Milly said you were on your way."

My rucksack slid to the floor and I jiggled my shoulders a few times to get the feeling back into them. Mum shut the door behind me.

"Did you call her?" I asked.

"I wondered if you were staying there for dinner and she said you'd just set off home." She turned back towards the kitchen and I followed.

"My rucksack was heavy. And my feet hurt."

"Milly said you'd been off on an adventure."

"Yeah. We went to the woods for a picnic."

Mum turned and smiled as she poured some water into a pan. "Did you have fun?"

I hesitated, then nodded. She raised an eyebrow at me.

"No, we did," I said. My shoulders were aching like mad, and so were my feet. "I'm just tired now, from the walk."

She cooked us dinner while I chatted about my homework and how the clearing in the woods looked now that summer was coming to a close. It was a relief to find that things weren't weird anymore, and we were soon talking like our argument this morning hadn't happened.

"Didn't you have anything to eat out there?" Mum asked.

I looked down at the huge second helping of pasta I'd just dumped on my plate. Then I grinned. "Yeah, but it was just health food stuff."

"Ahh." She nodded. "That was nice of Sandy."

I nodded, grinning as I tucked in. Mum watched me with half a smile on her face, her own plate empty, then asked me if I'd managed to finish all my homework.

"Just about, thank God," I said. "I had loads!" I took another bite of food, then shut my eyes and swore. Mum frowned at me. "Sorry, I just remembered – I left all my books at Milly's."

She laughed and stood up to take away the plates. "Never mind, you'll just have to pick them up tomorrow."

"Yeah," I agreed, thinking it would have to wait until the evening though. But I wasn't going to tell Mum that; she wouldn't like to know they were seeing my dad.

"I think I'm going to go read," I said, trying to hide a yawn as I spoke.

Mum wasn't fooled. "I don't know why you're so tired, but you need more rest" she said, coming over and cupping my face in her hands. "You look far too pale. Are you reading late at night or something?"

"I wish. I fall asleep as soon as I get into bed."

She looked at me for another second, and I thought she was

going to say something else, but she just nodded and let her hands run down my hair. "Off you go then. I'll bring you up some toast later, if you like?"

"Thanks," I said, getting up and yawning again.

"Mmm hmmm," she said, watching me go with her hands on her hips.

I hefted my rucksack back onto my shoulder and headed up the stairs. It was great to be back to normal with her again, I thought. Then I wondered if I could organise to have Milly come 'round here tomorrow evening. She could bring my home work with her and we could look at the book. A shiver of excitement ran through me. I knew what I would be doing tomorrow, and it was lucky Mum was going to be out because I didn't think she'd be that understanding about me looking up witches on the internet.

ELEVEN

That night, my dreams were full of colour and I woke up the next morning feeling like I'd slept on a cloud. My whole body felt transparent and full of light.

The sun was already showing through the gaps in my curtains, casting bright patches on the carpet, and downstairs I could hear Mum whistling as she got ready for work. She always worked on Sundays. Sometimes she could work from home, but today she was going into town to see some clients and do an auction; she wouldn't be home until the evening. Which meant, I thought with a smile, that I had the whole day to do what I liked.

I stretched out under the covers, enjoying the delicious feeling still lingering from my dreams. I couldn't remember anything specific from them – no images or words, just a feeling – but I hoped this was a sign that things were going to get better.

"Honey, I'm going to have to go in bit," Mum called up the stairs. "Do you want some breakfast now or will you do it yourself?"

"I'm coming now," I called back as I slipped out of bed

and into the warm patch of sunlight on the floor. My dressing gown was hanging behind the door and I pulled it on. Then I pulled open the door and padded downstairs on my bare feet.

"Good morning," I said, coming up behind her and giving her a hug. She turned to me and beamed, then gestured for me to sit down at the table.

"French toast," she said, putting down a plate in front of me. "And there's lunch in the fridge for later, so you don't have to do any cooking." She leaned out the kitchen to grab her coat, then began pulling it over her suit.

"Thanks, Mum," I said, tucking straight in.

She paused in the doorway, shaking her head at me. "I had no idea school could make you this tired. Or this hungry," she said. "You know, I came up to give you some supper last night but you were already fast asleep."

I shrugged, shoveling toast into my mouth as fast as I could then swallowing it in a huge gulp. "It must have been all that walking," I said, and she nodded.

"Well, I'll be on the usual number if you have any problems," she said, pulling on her handbag. "And Mrs. Busher is in next door if you need some company."

I nodded, swallowing another huge mouthful before getting up to give her a hug.

"I'll be fine," I said. "I was fine all summer, wasn't I?"

Mum hesitated, then nodded, brushing the hair out of my face. She looked pretty tired herself, I realised. I looked into her face and wondered why she was so worried all of a sudden. "Well, if you're sure," she said with a smile, and she gave me another squeeze before letting me go.

When I finished waving her goodbye from the door, I made myself another helping of French toast and carried it to the living room. The house was so quiet without her; it was kind of exciting. I had felt like this all summer too, waking up on the days I wasn't working to a whole day on my own. It was just the evenings alone I didn't like much.

I tried to decide what I was going to do today. There wasn't much point watching TV – there was never anything good on Sundays – but I could watch a video, or read, or even just go back to bed. I had to admit, that idea was tempting, and if I hadn't been so excited from my discoveries yesterday I probably would have just curled up with a book under the covers and dozed until lunchtime. But I had so many questions burning inside me, so much to investigate after Milly's revelations. There was no way I was going to be able to sleep just yet.

The idea that Grandma had been a witch, whatever that meant, was fantastic. I had never thought my family was anything special, especially Dad's side, but now there was something to get excited about. And from what Milly said yesterday, it was something amazing and kind of beautiful too; something worth learning more about.

As I finished up my breakfast, I wondered where Milly had started. How was I going to investigate this? Outside the kitchen window, the sun was filling up our little garden and making everything look fresh and alive. "Being in tune with nature," Milly had said. Where had she found that out?

I wished I'd asked her more questions yesterday, but I was pretty good at researching stuff too. I was going to have a good go at it myself before I met with her tonight. Hopefully that would help me understand what we were looking at in Grandma's book a bit better too, if we were lucky enough to get some time with it.

I sighed, feeling jumpy with impatience, and got up from the table to wash my breakfast things. I had forgotten all about the scary noises I'd heard on Friday, as well as the shadow that Milly and I had seen. But it all came back with a thud the moment I passed the dresser that sat just outside the kitchen door. There, right in the middle of it, sat the old, silver ring.

I stared, hardly daring to blink. How the hell had it gotten there? I had given it back to Mum, and I was sure she'd put it in her room; there was no way she'd leave it just lying around. With the sight of it, the memory of how I'd found it and the mystery about where it had come from returned vividly.

Without realising it, I'd been holding my breath. I tried to think – had it been there last night? Had Mum said anything about it? I reached out to touch it, then hesitated; I didn't want to move it, just in case Mum had put it there. There was no way I wanted her to think I'd stolen it from her room.

That was exactly what she was going to think, wasn't it? I told myself, pulling back my hand. If she hadn't put it there, she was going to think I'd moved it – what else could she think? I was angry. I had no idea what was going on, but it was definitely not funny. First Holly and Emily, and now Mum.

The horrible idea that someone was trying to mess with me sprung to mind. But who, and why? I shook my head, stepping away from the doorway and the dresser as I tried to calm down. There was no one in my life who would want to hurt me – at least that I knew of – and even if there was, how on earth would they make those noises, or that shadow, or move the ring without being in the house?

No, I was just feeling tired and stressed from last week. I was over-reacting. The noises on Friday had been some random plumbing sounds or something, and the shadow was the product of exhaustion. That was the only way to explain it.

I felt a bit better for deciding this and resolutely turned my back to the hallway without glancing at the ring again. I strode to the sink and turned on the kitchen radio, then concentrated on washing up for a while as my heart rate returned to normal. After five minutes of loud, upbeat music, I was feeling much better. I left the radio blaring behind me and walked upstairs, managing to laugh a little about how silly I'd been as I kept my eyes resolutely away from the dresser.

I spent the whole morning upstairs in my room, listening to music and surfing the internet. I took notes in my own journal, the one I wrote about my dreams in. It was usually hidden under the bed so Mum couldn't read it, so it was perfect for this little research project. I didn't need her finding out what I'd been researching. At least not yet.

It was surprisingly easy to find stuff out about witches – way easier than I'd thought. The trouble was more that there was so much information, and a lot of it seemed to be complete rubbish. I had to spend quite a lot of time sifting through pages to find the good bits.

At last, though, I found some good sites that seemed to match with everything Milly had said, as well as what felt right to me. That was a real surprise, because I'd never thought about anything like this before. But it was instantly clear to me what was true and what was just TV and film stuff. The right things were like a bell in my head: clear and easy to understand. By the time I was hungry, I had a good few pages of notes and was more than ready to turn off my computer and think about it all for a bit.

Downstairs, the radio was still playing and I sang along as I heated up my lunch, feeling excited and much more impressed by the whole idea than I had yesterday. I couldn't wait to talk to Milly about it.

I was so excited I felt like I was going to burst. The afternoon had dragged by, and at 5 o' clock I just couldn't wait any longer, so I called Milly's home phone. It took ages before someone picked up, and then all they said was, "What?"

I rolled my eyes. The low voice on the other end was clearly Toady, and I really didn't need any of his attitude. "Is Milly home yet?" I asked, keeping my fingers crossed.

"Nope," he said, "and she won't be until late."

I swore under my breath; I needed to get my homework at the least, even if we couldn't look at Grandma's book. "I need my books; I left them at your house."

"Oh well. I'm going out – you can't come and get them now."

"Fine," I said. I had to keep my temper or he'd get even worse. "Can you get her to call me when they get home?"

Toady didn't answer; I heard him snort, then the line went dead.

I swore again, this time out loud. I had no idea if he'd been telling the truth, but I couldn't call back now – not for an hour or so. Why did he have to be such a prat?

I sighed and put the phone back on the hook. It was just past five, and Mum would be home within the next hour and a half, so there wasn't much time for Milly to come 'round with the journal. We would just have to wait for another opportunity, I told myself, trying to pretend it wasn't such a big deal. But the thought of waiting for maybe a whole week made my stomach clench.

I didn't understand why it was such a big deal. What could be wrong with it that Sandy and my dad wanted to keep it from us? They were both pretty normal and laid back about most things; it wasn't like they were super religious or strict. I rolled my eyes and slid off the kitchen chair to head back upstairs, feeling let down and disappointed.

I had turned off the radio to make the phone call, and the house was silent again for the first time all day. It wouldn't normally bother me, but after the last few days, I noticed it; I shivered at the feeling and sped up towards the stairs.

My footsteps echoed a little in the cramped stairwell, and I felt my heart speed up. This is ridiculous, I told myself, trying to smile, but it didn't feel ridiculous; it felt creepy. And it didn't get any better. The longer the silence went on, the worse I felt. By the time I reached my bedroom door my palms were wet with sweat and I felt like I was going to jump out of my skin at the slightest thing. I hesitated as I pushed the wood back to reveal my room, unable to force myself to ignore the memory of the shadow. It had been around this time in the evening, I thought, and shuddered.

But there was nothing there; no shadow, no figure, and nothing had moved. I snorted. What the hell had gotten into me? Crossing the room, I sank onto my bed and put my feet up with a sigh. Mum would be home in a bit, so there wasn't much point doing any more research; I might as well just lie here and listen to music while I thought it all over.

I reached across and flicked on my stereo, letting the music wash over me. All the tension from the last few minutes as well as the last week began to dissolve. Everyone would think I was nuts if they knew how scared I'd gotten just from a quiet house. I laughed again and closed my eyes, and within minutes I was fast asleep.

TWELVE

I knew I was dreaming; my whole bedroom was just slightly off. There was light everywhere, but the window was dark and the lamps were all off. I got up from the bed, looking around. There was some reason I was here, I knew that, but I couldn't remember what it was.

The house was dead quiet. But I could feel that strange creeping feeling down my spine telling me someone else was nearby. I hesitated, then stepped across to the door. I had to know, I had to find out who it was; I pushed open the door and stepped out into the hallway.

The room behind me disappeared and I was surrounded by trees. I whirled around, trying to see how I'd gotten here, then reminded myself that I was dreaming. The light was fading. It was dusk in the forest, and beneath my bare feet there was snow thick enough to cover the scrubby underbrush with white.

I took another step forward. It struck me that the cold from the snow had no effect on me. And then I realised this forest was familiar, as though I'd been there before. But I couldn't have been. These rough, bare pines weren't anything like the leafy oaks and beeches of my favourite woods. Forests this vast and sparse didn't belong in England, I told myself. But still, I knew where to go without even thinking about it.

Setting off through the trees, I headed towards the place I needed to go. The light from the sky was fading now as the trees pressed closer, and the snow was falling so thick I couldn't see my feet. I felt guided forward; my feet found sure ground without even feeling for it. I walked on and on. It felt like forever, but I knew it was only minutes. I was asleep at home, after all, and Mum would be back soon to wake me. But time stretched between the trees, which cast a web of silence between their snowy branches.

It was only as the last of the light drained from between the tree trunks that I felt a sliver of ice like a cold, wet finger against the back of my neck. I whipped around, but there was no one there. The silence surrounded me, unbroken; I had heard no one move, no twigs crack and no snow crunch. I turned back to my path and carried on, my senses prickling. I could feel someone behind me just like I'd felt someone in the house. I kept on through the snow, placing my feet quickly but carefully with each step. It was easy, as though I'd walked this way a thousand times. I was nearly there; if I could just reach my destination before they caught up with me, I'd be okay.

My breath caught a little in my throat. The air was colder now, and bit into my face and lungs as I breathed, but I didn't dare slow down. I thought I heard a rustling behind me, and my heart leapt inside my chest, but I didn't turn around. The cold air billowed as I panted, steadying myself by pressing my palms against the rough bark of the tree trunks.

Then, as though someone had lit a bonfire, a light bloomed up ahead. I stumbled past the last few trees, forcing myself onward as cold fingers pulled at my shoulders and hair. I fell head first into the circle of warm light.

For a moment, there was a vision of something huge rearing before me in the dancing glow, and then the forest swam into darkness again and I was standing on the landing outside my bedroom door, my heart leaping as though it wanted to escape of chest. I gasped for breath, forgetting that I didn't need to breathe in a dream, and held my head in my hands to stop myself reeling. The air was still freezing cold. The house was silent as the forest. I wanted to go home now. I wanted to wake up, but I didn't know how.

I pushed open the bedroom door, ready to run back to where I knew my body was lying, to force myself awake, and then I felt my breath freeze in my lungs. The shadow was standing there, right in the middle of my room as though it had been waiting for me.

It's face turned towards me, a dark blankness, and it hung there. Still as stone, the coldness rippled from it. I wanted to scream, but there was no voice inside me. I wanted to run away, but my feet were numb with fear. A huge sound began, a tremendous, quaking roar that enveloped everything, and the house shook as though it was coming down around me.

In the middle of the room, the shadow flickered and jerked. The roar grew louder, vibrating through the walls and floor, up through my legs, and for a moment I wondered what new horror was about to burst out at me. And then it all disappeared.

In a single moment, the shadow vanished as though it had never been there. The roaring sound rose to almost deafening volume and then stopped, and I was stirring on my bed, rubbing my face.

I sat up and stared around me. The last light of day seeped out of the window, leaving the room a dark gold, and empty apart from me. I pressed my hands into my face and burst into tears. All I could think of was that I was going mad; I must be totally losing my mind. Then I realised what was missing: there was no music playing. My radio was turned off. How had that happened? It was so strange, and so inexplicable, that it jolted me out of my panic.

From the clock, I could see I'd only been asleep for 40 minutes. I shook my head and looked around the room, shivering.

The memory of my dream and that terrifying shadow figure in the middle of my room ran through me like an icicle, and I rubbed the tears from my face. I had no idea what was going on. But somehow, realising that something strange really was happening and it wasn't just me losing my mind, made me a feel a lot better.

I paused for a moment, steeling my nerves before I slid off the bed and onto the carpet. It was warm and dry, not frozen like in my dream. But still, I could feel that cold just at the edges of my awareness, like an echo. I peered at all my things, wondering if anything else had moved. My bag, my dropped clothes and my hairbrush were all where I had left them, and so were all my papers and notes on the desk. I took another ginger step towards the desk for a closer look and felt like I'd been punched in the guts. Right there, on top of all of the papers, was the old, green ring.

I stared at it, unable to move. For a moment, I felt like I was going to scream or just go running out of the house and into the street like a crazy woman. It was like the nightmare was still happening, like I hadn't woken up at all. I didn't need to ask how it had gotten there, I knew; that shadow figure had put it there, and it was watching me even now.

I felt sick. I didn't know what I should do. I didn't think there was anything I could do. Something was in my house; it was messing with me, and no one else in the world was going to believe me. I had to pull myself together, because if I panicked that was it. I didn't know what would happen if I did lose control, but I knew without even thinking about it that it would be bad.

Forcing myself to take a deep breath, I raised my head. I could feel that shiver of cold just out of my reach, and I knew what it was now. Repressing a shudder, I reached out and picked up the ring with trembling fingers. It lay cool and solid in my palm, just like any other piece of jewellery. But I wasn't fooled.

Then the front door banged open downstairs and I jumped, almost dropping the ring back onto the desk.

"I'm home!" Mum's voice came up the stairs, breaking the silence of the house and sending little ripples through the stillness and the cold that had been enveloping me.

I let go of the breath that had been burning in my chest and stuffed the ring deep into my jeans pocket. I'd have to deal with it later.

"Coming!" I shouted back.

I set my shoulders back, took a deep breath and swept out of the bedroom without another glance.

THIRTEEN

Despite my worries, nothing out of the ordinary happened once Mum was home. The house was quiet and warm, and we had dinner together without anything a flicker of that weird coldness interrupting us. I said good night at 9 o'clock, my tummy full of butterflies again; the thought of having to face Holly and Emily at school the next morning was nerve wracking enough to replace the strange shadow in the forefront of my mind.

Mum kissed me goodnight and I hurried off. Whatever else might have been going on, and whatever was coming in the weeks ahead, I got a peaceful night's sleep, full of rainbow-filled dreams that melted once I opened my eyes to the bright Monday morning.

However, it wasn't the best of weeks for me. I hadn't been able to pick up my homework on Sunday evening, so I got into trouble with my teachers on Monday morning. Then the weather turned on Monday afternoon, and by the time I had to walk home it was pouring, drenching me and the books I did have with me before I got even halfway home.

I walked home that day, and every day that week, on my

own; Emily and Holly still refused to talk to me, and no one else walked my way.

It was pretty miserable, and if it hadn't been for the mystery of Grandma's journal and the quick chats I managed to snatch with Milly at school, I would have been feeling desperate by the time Friday came round.

One thing that did help was my new certainty that I wasn't going 'round the twist. The occasional odd noise at home when I was by myself was much less worrying now that I knew it was real and I had a plan to figure out what was going on. The shadowy figure didn't show up again, which was a big relief; I wondered whether my confidence in my own sanity was the reason it wasn't around as much, as though it wasn't worth it if it couldn't scare me half to death.

Mum was away as much as usual those evenings and I spent a large amount of my time doing more research on witchcraft and all its variations, hoping to find something that might help me understand what was going on. There was a lot about protection spells and things like that, but somehow the thought of doing a spell didn't feel right. I decided it would be better to wait and see what Grandma's journal said instead of meddling where I had no idea what I was doing.

I was glad I waited. By Friday evening, desperate to get together with Milly, I called her up as soon as I got home, keeping my fingers crossed she'd pick up.

"Hi!" I heard Milly's voice and broke out in a relieved grin.

"Hi," I said. "I'm so glad you're there. Can we meet up?"

Milly laughed. In the background, I could hear the TV and Toady talking over it at the top of his voice.

"I think so," she said, "but it'll have to be tomorrow – and I do have homework to do as well."

"Will you come here? Mum'll be around, but she won't

bother us."

The was a pause while Milly thought about it. "Yeah, I think that would be best." She hesitated before continuing. "And I think we have to do it sooner rather than later."

I didn't ask her what she meant; the slight twisting in my stomach told me she'd found something about the shadow, but there was no way she could talk about it on the phone while her family were in the room. I'd just have to wait one more night to find out.

"Okay," I said, twiddling the phone cord. "Can you come 'round early then?"

"I'll be there by nine," she said, and there was another burst of laughter in the background. "I'd better go," she added, then whispered, "don't worry about it though, okay?"

I nodded, then realised she couldn't see me. "Yeah," I said, "see you tomorrow."

We said goodbye and hung up. I felt a little lonely, turning back to my empty house after hearing Milly's home full of noise and laughter. It sounded like Toady had friends 'round, and Milly was just about old enough to hang with them now. A flash of annoyance ran through me, leaving me clenching my fists, and I forced myself to relax again. It was just the way it was and there was nothing I could do about it, but I'd give anything for brothers and sisters. Or even just to have my school friends back.

I rolled my eyes and sighed. There was no use brooding over it; they'd come around eventually. It seemed even more ridiculous now, thinking about what we'd fallen out over. But, like with most arguments, we'd all said some pretty stupid things by now and it would take some time to cool down.

I grabbed my school bag off the floor and began to trudge up the stairs. Mum had warned me she'd be more late than usual that night, leaving me a plate of dinner in the fridge and some desert to warm up and eat on my own. That meant I'd be there on my own for hours that evening, in the dark after the sun had gone down; it was the first time I'd spent so long alone there since Sunday's craziness.

The house felt empty, and I couldn't feel any of the coldness that I always noticed when something strange was going to happen. But the silence of the house, with the light outside already starting to fade, sent a shiver through me. I hurried into my room to put on some music. I did not want to sit in that silence, waiting for something to happen.

With the radio playing nice and loud and all my lights on, it was much more relaxing in my room. It was almost as though nothing strange had been happening at all, I thought, looking around at how normal everything was. If it wasn't for the old ring hidden at the bottom of my desk drawer, I could almost forget it all right then and there and feel like a normal person.

But I knew the ring was there; it rattled every time I opened the drawer to get a pen, reminding me of its weird existence and how it had moved all by itself. I still hadn't figured out where it had come from, what to tell Mum if she asked about it, or what it was all about; just looking at it gave me the creeps, so I left it buried there under all my stuff, hoping that one day it would just disappear again.

Forcing myself to stop thinking about it, I powered up my laptop and got myself comfortable. I wanted to get as much homework done as possible tonight so I could concentrate on Grandma's diary tomorrow. But it had been a long week, and I was exhausted. The back of my head was aching too, and my bed was looking tempting.

I sighed, trying to focus on what I needed to work on. I had never known biology could be so complicated before, with all these Latin names I had to remember. I had a test next week, and I'd already done badly on my first homework assignment. It wouldn't help to skip this one too.

I rubbed my eyes. The headache was getting worse – worse than it had been all week. Maybe I needed glasses, I wondered, pushing my fingers against my face to relieve the throbbing. I was so tired. It had to be illegal to be this tired, I thought to myself, wondering if I should get some paracetamol.

The room began to spin. I gripped the desk to steady myself, but the room kept spinning, faster and faster. It was making me feel sick, so I closed my eyes, hoping it would pass. I'd never been this tired in my life; I longed for my bed.

I couldn't think straight with the room spinning like this and my head thumping and my eyes refusing to open. No, this wouldn't do; I couldn't get any homework done like this. I'd just have to rest for a little bit and try again later, I decided, pushing myself onto my feet so I could lie down.

The room lurched beneath me. I couldn't see any more; everything was fading, falling away beneath me. I thought for a moment I might be sick, and then everything went dark and quiet, and I stopped thinking anything.

�

Something was snuffling, right next to me in the dark. I wondered if I was still in my bedroom, then dismissed the idea. It was daylight when I'd gone to bed, I thought, it couldn't be late enough to be pitch black now.

That made sense, so I decided I was dreaming. The thought didn't worry me; at least I was getting some rest. I had been so, so tired. Maybe I was ill, I wondered, enjoying the soft darkness

I lay in. It felt comfortable and warm here, and the quiet, animal noises nearby didn't worry me either; after all, I was dreaming.

After a while, I decided to sit up. As I did, a soft light bloomed and flickered up ahead. I sat and watched it, wondering where it had come from. It was beautiful, and growing brighter as I watched. Then there were other lights as well – tiny points of silver up ahead where the ceiling should have been.

Beneath my hands I could feel cool, gravelly stone, a bit like coarse sand. There was a breeze, gentle and cool, and with a hint of wood smoke in it. I yawned and got to my feet.

"Hello," said a familiar voice, making me jump. I hadn't thought there was anyone else in the dark with me.

I looked around. "Who's there?"

"Come over to the fire," the voice said. There was a slight scuffing noise, as though something was shifting its weight on the stony ground, and the snuffling grew a little louder.

I felt strange; the little knot of tension I'd been carrying around in my stomach all week was looser. This place was like a memory, something I'd known well and then forgotten.

The voice didn't speak again, and I knew they were waiting for me to make my decision. And deep down, in the place dream-knowing comes from, I knew this was where I needed to be. This was the place I'd been trying to reach in all my dreams for the last two weeks.

I hesitated for only one more moment, steeling myself for what might come next, ready to run if I needed to. Then I took a few steps forward, closer to the warm, flickering light. It came more clearly into view, resolving like a kaleidoscope into a bright wood fire on a dark, stone floor. I stared, watching the flames leap and dance in wild patterns. Nothing else moved; no one spoke. I waited, wondering what was going to happen, then took another step forward.

Now the snuffling, rumbling noise was louder. It vibrated up through my legs from my feet and reminded me of someone snoring. Dark silhouettes formed in the shadows around the fire and I peered at them, trying to make out who was there.

"Welcome," said the voice more clearly now. I frowned, trying to remember where I'd heard it before; it was so familiar to me, soft and rich as honey, but cracked too, as though by age.

"Do I know you?" I asked, peering hard into the shadows.

The fire leapt higher, sending sparks up into the air above us, like dancing stars, and for a moment I glimpsed two figures on the other side of the fire – one small, one huge – and I gasped at the sight of them.

But something was wrong; the ground lurched beneath my feet, cracking with the sound of striking lightening. The shapes stirred, thrown back into darkness as the fire went out with a hiss. I reached for them, trying to step forward, trying to hear what they were saying as they hurtled away from me.

I was falling, backwards and downwards, through the darkness that had no stars. Everything was upside down and inside out. I felt like I was being pulled apart, and then squashed up tight – so tight I couldn't breathe. And then, suddenly, there was blinding light and lots of noise and I was gasping and choking, trying to sit up while strong hands gripped my shoulders.

FOURTEEN

I blinked into the light, trying to figure out who all the people were.

"Relax."

The hands on my shoulders held me firmly, stopping me from sitting up. I brought my hands up to bat them away, but they just gripped me tighter.

"She's confused," someone said.

Another person came up close to me and took my hand. "Just lie still, honey," Mum's voice said, and her face resolved out of the blur.

"Mum?" I said. I was starting to feel frightened. "What's going on?"

"It's okay," she said, stroking my forehead. I tried to shake her off.

My eyes were working better now and the room around me focused into my own bedroom, full of strangers in uniforms. I was lying on the floor. I realised what must have happened.

"What do you remember?" one of the men said, still holding my shoulder as he studied my face. I swallowed, trying to figure out what to tell them and what to leave out; it was hard to think with all this light and noise after the peaceful place I'd just been in.

"I, err," I began, rubbing my face with my other hand and letting them sit me up against the bed. "I was tired, and my head hurt – I was going just to lie down for a bit." I glanced up at the bed. "I guess I didn't make it to the bed," I said, with a shaky laugh.

The man sat back on his heels and shook his head. "No," he said, "you didn't. Looks like you passed out en route."

He was checking my eyes with a light now, while his partner filled out forms on a big pad.

I turned to Mum. "I'm sorry," I said, and the tears filling her eyes spilled out onto her cheeks.

"Don't be stupid," she said, wiping them away. "It's not your fault. I was just so worried." She hugged me like I was a piece of glass.

The other paramedic looked down at his notes and then leaned forward to talk to me. "Did you eat enough today, do you think?"

I nodded.

"She's been so hungry lately," Mum said. "You couldn't stop her from eating."

He nodded and made another note. "And you haven't banged your head at all?"

I shook my head and they wrote some more things down.

"Well, it could just be a bad reaction to the flu or exhaustion, but seeing as you've been unconscious for a while, I'd like you to come in for some tests to be sure."

My insides flipped; I had to be at home to see Milly tomorrow. This was not how I imagined spending my weekend.

The man noticed my face and gave me a sympathetic smile.

"I know it's a pain," he went on, "but it's important we

make sure nothing else is going on. You could be back home tonight."

Mum was nodding; she already had her 'getting organised' face on. I sighed; I wasn't going to be able to get out of this.

"I'm feeling okay now," I said. But the ambulance men were already checking their equipment and radioing into the hospital. Nobody heard me.

"I'll grab you some books and stuff," Mum said, giving my arm a squeeze and getting up off the floor. I watched her go, feeling queasy with guilt. This was exactly the kind of trouble I didn't want to cause her.

Within the space of five minutes, Mum and the paramedics packed into the ambulance and we were on our way to the hospital. Things just couldn't get any weirder, I thought to myself, but there was no way I was going to tell any doctors that.

It was just my luck to pass out on a Friday night; the emergency department was packed. Fortunately, being brought in on an ambulance helped speed things along and by the time I was starting to feeling tired we had already had the tests they needed and were seeing the doctor again.

"Well," she said, glancing at the results and giving Mum a reassuring smile. "We can see there's no head trauma, and all your blood tests were fine as well." She smiled at me, then continued. "I think it's most likely you just had a blood pressure drop, probably from lack of food or dehydration. And then you banged your head as you fell – which explains why you remained unconscious for a little while."

Mum nodded, giving me a relieved look and squeezing my hand. "Is there anything we need to watch for?" she asked.

I let my mind drift. I already knew why I'd passed out, and the doctor wasn't going to be able to stop it happening again.

I had to talk to Milly about how to put a stop to this, before it caused Mum any more trouble.

"No," the doctor was saying, "just make sure she rests for 24 hours, keep an eye on her through the night and come back if it happens again."

She was up and gone before Mum had time to reply; the corridor outside my curtain was filling up again, and the nurses had already called for her twice. We looked at each other, then began to gather up our stuff. It had taken over three hours to be told that everything was fine, and I was exhausted again. Mum gave me a pale smile as she helped me off the bed.

"Does your head hurt?" she asked, guiding me past the crowd of waiting patients and their grumbling families.

I shrugged; it was a little tender where it had hit the floor, but nothing some paracetamol wouldn't sort out. She squeezed my arm, and we made our way out of the stuffy hospital and into the car park. Mum sighed, looking around. "I suppose we'll have to get a taxi."

She started digging in her bag for her phone and led me away from the entrance to the pickup area where some cars were waiting with their engines on. I followed, trying to keep up. My head swam, and I told myself to keep breathing and not pass out again – I definitely wouldn't get home for tomorrow if I did that. But just as we stopped to wait for the taxi, another car pulled up next to us and honked its horn. Mum glanced at it, then looked again. A grimace flashed across her face.

I followed her gaze and my heart sank at the sight of my dad's silver Mercedes idling beside the curb. Mum and I caught each other's eye, then stepped over to the waiting car and pulled open the doors.

"Good timing, huh?" Dad said, giving me a grin as he waved us inside. I slid into the back seat and pulled my bag in behind me.

"How did you know I was here?" I asked. From the backseat, I watched him eye Mum through his thick glasses as she got into the passenger seat. He looked older and a bit greyer than when I'd last seen him, but he had a new baby now.

"I called him," Mum answered. "When you were having the scan. Thought he should know what had happened." She turned to him as he pulled out into the road.

"You didn't have to come all this way," she said, clutching her bag with both hands in her lap.

He shrugged. "It wasn't that far," he said, glancing over his shoulder at me. "And I wanted to make sure you're all right."

I tried to smile, but my head was throbbing again. I rubbed the place where I'd banged it. "Just a bit tired. And sore," I said.

"Well, I'll get you home a.s.a.p. and you can get some rest. I suppose it's just exhaustion from your first few weeks at school, huh?"

I shrugged, and Mum gave him a weak smile.

"How's the little one doing?" she asked. I winced and ducked my head down so they didn't see, but neither of them were looking at me.

"She's fine; we're all fine."

The atmosphere in the car stiffened and I closed my eyes to block the whole crazy situation out.

I didn't listen to the rest of their conversation. I knew they were being so polite because I was there, and I appreciated it, but I would have preferred it if they didn't talk at all. At least the hospital wasn't far from home; we were pulling up outside the house within 15 minutes of Dad picking us up.

He got out of the car to say goodbye to me while Mum opened the front door. Feeling even more awkward than usual, I thanked him for the ride and promised to come and see him soon. He grinned and tried to joke with me, but thankfully Mum was there to usher me inside. My eyelids were heavy and all I could think of was getting into bed.

I heard them saying a cool goodnight as I dragged myself up the stairs to my room. I was too tired to care; within seconds, I was undressed and falling onto my bed. And in another second, I was fast asleep.

FIFTEEN

I felt so much better the next morning. My headache was gone and all I had left to remind me of the previous night's adventure was a tender bump behind my ear. Thankfully, Mum had relaxed a bit overnight and was almost back to normal as she made me breakfast and told me what had happened.

"I just found you there, right on the bedroom floor," she said, watching me with her head in her hands. "I thought my heart would stop – it was that frightening."

I gave her a smile.

"Thank goodness I was home earlier than I planned or you could have lain there for hours," she went on, and I heard the tearfulness in her voice again.

"Yeah, but I didn't, did I?" I said. "And I'd probably have woken up then anyway – it's not like they did anything to wake me up, did they? I'd have just woken up with a headache. That's all."

I pulled a funny face and rubbed the sore spot on my head, making her laugh.

"I suppose," she agreed, nodding and wiping her eyes. Then she laughed again. "I can't believe your father drove all that way!"

I looked at her, trying to figure out what she wanted to hear. But she didn't wait for me to answer.

"It was nice of him, though," she said, giving me a smile and patting my free hand. I shrugged. "Milly was going to come over today," I said, changing the subject. "Can she still come 'round ? We've got homework to do."

Mum hesitated.

"I'll take it easy," I interrupted before she could say no. "I promise – we'll just sit in my room and do our homework and chat. Okay?"

She paused for another second and I held my breath, then she nodded. "Okay," she said, holding my gaze, "but if I hear any messing about, she'll have to go home. Got it? You're supposed to be resting today."

I nodded, trying to look more relaxed than I was. I didn't think she'd consider getting excited very restful. Inside I was dancing with glee; I was going to start getting to the bottom of this, I was sure. Milly had definitely found something that would make it all clear.

I tried my best to move around slowly and be quiet while I waited for Milly to arrive. Mum was keeping a close watch on me, and I knew if I put one foot wrong, that would be that. My stomach turned at the thought; I knew if I didn't sort this out soon, I'd get into the same state I did last night and end up back in the hospital. And then they'd figure out that I was seeing crazy stuff, and all hell would break loose. No, I told myself, I'm not going to let that happen.

I was up in my room when the doorbell rang, and I made myself sit and wait so Mum could open the door. Rushing down the stairs wasn't resting either, in her books. I listened as she greeted Milly and told her what had happened last night, then I grinned as she gave her strict instructions not to wind me up.

Milly was the picture of understanding, from what I heard; she was always good at talking to grownups. Mum was satisfied, anyway, because it wasn't long before Milly's footsteps were on the stairs and she was pushing open my bedroom door and giving me a double thumbs-up. She dropped her bag onto the floor, then came and sat next to me on the bed.

"So," she said. "I hear you had an adventure last night – are you all right?"

I rolled my eyes and told her what had happened, or at least the quick version. She listened, her eyes narrowing a little.

"You didn't just get too hungry, did you?" she asked.

I shook my head. "No. Why does everyone ask that? It's not like I'm a horse or something!"

Milly snorted.

"No, it was the same feeling as before; like my head was going to explode with pressure. And there was something here, something I couldn't see..." I shook my head again, trying to remember. "And there's something else," I said, leaning in and glancing at the door. Milly held up her finger and slid off the bed. She tiptoed across the room to the door and listened for a moment.

"I can't hear her," she whispered. "Just wait a minute."

I nodded, watching as she swung the door open a little and tiptoed into the hallway.

"Hi!" she said, and I knew she'd been spotted. "Can we have something to drink, please?"

I heard her footsteps get louder as Mum joined her. She must have been in her bedroom, I thought. Thank God Milly had the sense to check.

"Sure, what would you like?"

I listened as Milly asked for milkshakes and then chatted all the way downstairs to the kitchen. I smiled as I heard the radio turn on, wondering if that was Milly too. I slid off the bed to pull my journal and all my notes out from under my mattress, hoping the radio would mask the noise I made.

Then I was back on my bed with my papers safely tucked under the covers and Milly was climbing back up the stairs with two milkshakes. I grinned as she came into the room and swung the door shut behind her with her foot.

"Here," she said, handing me a cool glass.

"Thanks. Nice one with the radio."

She grinned. "Thought it might help, and your Mum loves that station," she said. "She was in her room – good thing I checked."

I nodded, wondering if Mum would have been more worried about whispering than she was about me getting too lively. We picked up our glasses and sipped at them, not talking for a moment as we made sure it was safe to go on. Mum was singing along downstairs with no sign of coming back up.

"Okay," Milly said, putting down her glass on my desk and leaning forward so we wouldn't be overheard. "What were you going to tell me?"

I wondered how to explain it; I'd never had to put anything like this into words before. "Well," I began, scrunching up my eyes and trying to remember the details. "When I passed out, I had a dream. It was really vivid – a bit like the ones I've been having recently, but even more real. And I knew I was dreaming."

I held on tight to the cool glass in my hands as I spoke. It seemed as I spoke that the dream world came closer and I felt like I needed an anchor to stop me from slipping away again.

"I was somewhere dark, but it wasn't scary. Not this time

anyway. It was like I supposed to be there, like it was somewhere I'd been before. There was a fire up ahead, like a camp fire. And there were... I think they were people… with me in the darkness."

Milly's eyes were wide. "What kind of people?" she whispered.

I closed my eyes and tried to envision them. "I couldn't see them properly, not at first. But one of them spoke to me in a woman's voice. I thought I recognised it."

I looked at her. She was watching me with a fierce, hungry look. "You don't think I'm crazy, do you?" I said.

"No. Grandma's journal talks about stuff like this."

I nodded, feeling a bit lighter.

"What else?" Milly asked.

"So there was that one voice, and there was also another noise, like a snuffling sound. And there were shapes on the other side of the fire – one small and one big. Really big."

Milly nodded as she turned her eyes from me. She looked really serious, and way older than me in that moment. A jolt went through my stomach; I had no idea what I was doing or what was going on.

"Do you understand any of this?" I asked.

"I haven't got a clue." She turned back to me and broke into a smile. "But don't worry, we'll figure it out."

I nodded, swallowing the tightness in my throat. "But why do you think this is happening to me? Why now?"

She didn't answer me at first; her eyes went back to my window and the bright sky beyond it. Then she said, "I don't know. We need to find out more before we can figure that out."

"You don't think it could be because of Grandma's journal?" I remembered how this had all started just before I first heard about it. But Milly shook her head.

"No, I don't think so," she said. "That doesn't feel like it to me – does it to you?"

I sighed and covered my face with my hands. "I don't know – I don't know what I feel right now, to be honest. I'm just so tired. And worried."

With my eyes closed, I felt the bed beneath me shift and then Milly's arms wrapping around my shoulders. She gave me a hard squeeze and I felt safer than I had all week.

"It's okay," she whispered. "We're going to sort this out."

I nodded into my palms. "I'm just really, really tired. That's the problem," I said through my fingers. "I don't feel like I sleep anymore. I just dream."

"Look at me."

I looked up and let my hands fall into my lap. Milly's brown eyes held mine, and her hands firmly held my shoulders as she spoke.

"You are okay, and we are going to sort this out," she said, emphasising every word. I wasn't sure I believed her, but I nodded anyway.

"Okay?"

"Okay," I agreed, forcing myself to smile.

"Good. So the first thing we need to do is go through Grandma's journal for anything that seems relevant – agreed?"

I sat up straighter and brushed my eyes. Milly was right and I knew it; I had to stop worrying and do something.

Milly reached down and pulled her bag up onto the bed beside us. "I brought it with me," she said, reaching into the bag and rummaging around through all her stuff.

"Thank you."

I couldn't help smiling; she looked so excited at what we were doing that it made everything seem easier to deal with. She grinned back at me and pulled the old red book out of the depths of her bag.

"Here," she said, laying it in my lap. "I've already had a bit of a read when Mum's been asleep in the evenings. There are some things I want to show you."

She began to turn the pages. My stomach did a little flip as I remembered how serious she sounded on the phone last night, and I wondered what she'd found.

"There," she said, pointing to one of the pages, "read that."

The page was old, thin with time, and marked with smudges as though dirty fingers had poured over it time and again. The writing was the same as on the first page, elegant and dense, written in pencil. Every inch of the page was covered in it except for one corner.

For a few moments I just stared, taken aback by the little pencil drawing and forgetting to read. There, as clear as if I'd drawn it myself, was a beautiful, accurate study of the ring I'd found in my bag. There was no colour in the drawing, but the markings and the shape were exactly the same. I felt my face flush, my mind tumbled with all sorts of ideas.

"Does that look familiar?" Milly asked after I'd sat there in silence for at least a minute without reading. I nodded, speechless. More than anything else I'd seen or read, this confirmed the truth for me; what I was experiencing was real, and my Grandma had known about this stuff too.

"Read what it says," Milly insisted, pointing to the first paragraph. I blinked, then followed her finger and began to read.

"I made the ring with silver and a small green stone that I found at the river bank over 20 years ago. It has the symbol of Tierne carved on the inside, as he instructed me. I don't know how or why I am to use it, but I trust the Spirits – they have never lead me wrong yet."

I swallowed, trying to take in the words. It was like a voice coming back to me through time, a voice from so early in my childhood that it lived only in my dreams. Finally, I knew where I had heard the voice from my vision last night.

"It was Grandma," I said, turning to Milly. "It was Grandma in my dream last night. She was on the other side of the fire."

Milly's eyes widened, but I didn't wait for her to speak.

"She must have made the ring herself – for this Tierne person – and now, somehow, it's come to me."

"But how do you know it was her?"

"I just know. I recognised her voice," I said, knowing it didn't make any sense, but that it was true anyway.

Milly hesitated, glancing at the journal. "That is the ring, isn't it?" she said, looking back up at me. I nodded; my whole body felt hot and itchy with excitement.

"Yeah, it's definitely it – look," I said, leaning over and pulling the old ring from my desk drawer. It lay on my palm in the sunlight, battered and stained with age, but unmistakably the same ring that was drawn on the page in my lap. Looking closer at it than I ever had before, I could even make out a worn inscription on the inside of the band; a few wavy lines that looked, if I squinted my eyes, like some kind of animal.

"You see," I said, turning back to Milly and holding out the ring to her. She peered at it without picking it up, then looked into my eyes.

"It does seem to be the same, yes," she said, her voice halting. I felt a surge of impatience go through me. Why was she doubting this?

"It was you that brought me the book; you thought it was the same as well," I said, trying to keep my voice even.

Milly frowned. "I know," she said. "I just – I don't understand how you can know it was Grandma in your dream. That's all."

She put her hand on my knee.

"I'm scared for you," she said so quietly that I almost couldn't hear her. "I've never seen you like this before. And after all that's been going on, I just don't want us to make a mistake."

That quenched my impatience. We couldn't hurry this. "You're right," I said, nodding. "It just feels so true. That's all." I dropped the ring onto the book and tried to relax. "But I'll not make my mind up yet – not before we investigate some more. Okay?"

Milly stared at the ring for a minute, biting her lip. "Yeah."

I looked down at the book to read on. The paragraph below the drawing of the ring was even more interesting.

"I will empower it tonight, which is the dark moon, at the clearing in the forest. Tierne said he would meet me there and show me what to do next. After 15 years of walking this path, it still amazes me how events just seem to fit together, even here in this land that has fallen asleep. But tonight, I will return to the forest of my homeland."

I read to the end, drinking it all in. The forest – that was familiar too, but what did she mean about the land having 'fallen asleep'? "What do you think of this?" I said, pointing to the paragraph.

"I think she was here, in England, when she wrote it. She must have been talking about the homeland she'd left during the war."

"But what about the bit about the land being asleep? Do you understand what she meant?"

"No. Maybe."

I looked up and raised an eyebrow. Milly looked uncomfortable, but she went on.

"It fits with some of the research I've done – lots of people talk about the land, the trees, all of nature as though it's alive, just like us. I suppose something that's alive can be asleep..."

We looked at each other and a charge tingled up and down my spine.

"But how could she get from this country to that forest in one night?"

Milly shook her head. "I have no idea. She can't have actually gone back to Finland, can she? Not in time to get back for morning. She had children at home."

I stared at her. She was right, but then what had Grandma meant?

Turning back to the page, I scanned for any explanation, but she went on to describe how she'd made the ring instead.

"Have you read all the bits before this?" I asked, looking at how many pages were before this one. Milly shook her head and shrugged, looking a bit sheepish.

"I just... I don't know..." she said, waving her hands around as she tried to explain. "I suppose I just opened it where I felt like I had to look. I can't describe it."

I shook my head at her in disbelief, but I couldn't stop myself from giggling. This was totally, absolutely nuts, but it was pretty cool too.

"Anne!" Mum's voice came up the stairs, popping the bubble of silence around us like a pin. Milly and I jumped, and I shushed her under my breath as I slid off the bed and padded over to the door.

"Yeah, Mum?"

"What's all this giggling I can hear?" she yelled, and I heard her footsteps start up the stairs. I turned back to Milly and gestured wildly; she crammed my journal, the notes and Grandma's book under the covers as fast as she could, then sat on them.

"Sorry," I said, turning back to Mum as she came up onto the landing. "Got a bit carried away."

She nodded, trying to look stern, but I could tell she wasn't really angry. "Well, you're supposed to be resting, so tone it down a bit," she said, wagging a finger at me. Then she smiled. "It's nearly lunchtime anyway – do you want me to bring something up?"

"It's all right, Auntie Jo," Milly said as she stepped out into the hallway behind me. "I can make us something if you like."

Mum blinked for a moment, then smiled at her. "That would be great, Milly. Thank you," she said, then she gave us another piercing look. "You're sure you're not up to something in there, something you don't want me to see?" she asked. Milly laughed.

"No," I said, as Milly swung the door wide so Mum could see the whole room.

"See? I'm doing what I'm supposed to," I said, rolling my eyes.

"Okay. Just keep the noise down." She turned away and started back down the stairs. "And make sure you eat something soon," she called from the bottom step.

Milly and I turned to each other and I resisted letting out a huge sigh of relief. Milly waved me back to the bed and pushed the door closed to behind her.

"That was close!" I whispered. Milly nodded, putting her hand over her mouth and going pink. I looked away – we were just going to make each other laugh again if we weren't careful. Between the wild feeling that all this new information was giving me and the close call with Mum, I was having a hard time staying calm.

After a few moments of taking deep breaths, Milly pulled the door open again. Then she pointed at me.

"Get back into bed. I'm going to make some sandwiches,"

she said. "What do you want in yours?"

"Peanut butter," I said, collapsing back onto my elbows and watching her go. It was ridiculous, all this fuss over me, but I did feel pretty tired if I was honest with myself. I stared out of the window, wondering why this had all happened now, but no answers came to me. I pulled Grandma's journal out from under my covers and leafed through it again.

There were so many interesting pages, so many new ideas to explore. I couldn't wait to finish reading one page before I turned to another, back and forth, from the front to the back of the book, letting it open where the pages wanted. It was truly amazing; there was so much in here that I'd never even imagined before. Beautiful sketches of trees and people and animals and some things I didn't recognise at all, poems and songs written out in her lovely handwriting, long pages of notes that were so tightly written I almost had to touch the pages with my nose to read them. It was a treasure trove, something wholly ours.

I poured through the pages, only half-reading them, until Milly came back up the stairs with a tray teetering with sandwiches and drinks. She flashed a grin at me as she pushed the bedroom door shut behind her with her heel, then put the tray down on the bed.

"What have you found?" she asked, swinging the chair around from the desk to sit on. I looked down at the journal in my lap, letting my hands leaf through the pages by themselves, as thought they could absorb what was written on them just by running over the writing.

"Bits and pieces. I haven't been reading it; just looking," I said, taking a sandwich in my free hand.

She nodded. "It does seem to have a mind of its own, doesn't it?" she said, giving me a funny look. But I knew what she meant.

"Yeah, it has a pattern. Like an order it wants to be read in, or something..." I said, looking back down at it as I chewed.

Milly nodded, looking thoughtful. "Grandma's letter said it had everything in it we would need to learn about her and what she did. It does seem to have much more detail than anything I've found online, or anything I've read in any books, either. There are things in there I've never even heard of before – like when she talked about going back to the forest of her homeland, even though she was in this country."

I nodded; it was so mysterious, but for the first time in weeks I felt like something made sense. It felt like I was on the right track.

We ate in silence for while, each of in our own thoughts. I let mine wander, not paying attention until I realised I was going over and over the same idea. I put down my glass.

"Do you think there's something in here about that shadow I've been seeing?"

The question broke Milly out of her thoughts and she looked up at me. "I'm not sure. I haven't seen anything about a shadow yet," she said, "but that doesn't mean it's not in there."

We looked at the book, sitting next to me on the bed just like any other journal. It was interesting to learn about Grandma and all her beautiful beliefs, but what did it matter if I couldn't change what was happening to me?

"Maybe they don't have anything to do with each other?"

Milly shook her head. "I don't think that's true – I mean, there's the timing, for one thing. They did kind of come into your life at the same time, didn't they?"

I shrugged. I wasn't convinced that meant anything.

"And then," she went on before I could interrupt, "there's the fact that Grandma talks so much about spirits, and she describes similar stuff in there to what you've told me as well."

"Like what?"

"Like noises with no cause, and stuff moving on its own," she said, reaching for the book and turning through the pages again. "I know I saw something about stuff like that somewhere."

I watched her turn the pages, my stomach starting to do back-flips. I hadn't realised before, or maybe it just hadn't been there, but I was starting to feel that strange pressure in my head again. And just on the edges of my senses, like in a dream, there was a growing coldness as though snow was falling all around me, just out of sight.

I shivered a little and hugged myself, trying to push the feeling away. I didn't want to pass out again and lose this chance to figure out what was going on. No one but Milly would understand – anyone else would think I'd lost it, even Mum.

I had to find out what Grandma had known, what she had seen. It was the only think I could think of that might help me.

I blinked, trying to ignore the throbbing that was building in my skull. Then I leaned forward to try and see the pages as Milly turned through them. She didn't seem to be going through them in any order, but back and forth randomly.

"Why don't you ask it?" I asked without thinking. It was as though the words had come from someone else, through the blanket of pain and coldness that was starting to smother me. Milly glanced up at me.

"That's a good idea," she said, peering at me. Then she frowned. "Are you all right?"

I nodded, forcing myself to stop shivering. She hesitated, then looked back down at the journal.

"Okay," she said, "here goes." Her voice faltered a little as she spoke down at the book. "Can you show me the page about strange noises and things moving..." she said, glancing up at me for reassurance, "please?"

We looked at each other and I nodded for her to go on. The pain in my head was roaring now, pulsing with my heartbeat, and I could barely keep my eyes open to watch her as she allowed the book to fall open between her palms.

"No way!" she gasped, looking up at me and grinning. Her finger pointed to the top of the left page, one of the earliest in the journal. "This is it," she said, turning back to it and shaking her head. "This is exactly the page I read before – the one I told you about."

I blew out a breath and nodded, finally allowing my eyes to close as the darkness behind them threatened to swallow me up. But I held on, clenching my hands around the base of the bed and fighting to stay upright.

From a long way away, I heard Milly say my name, asking me if I was all right. I couldn't speak though; I couldn't even move – all of my energy was going into staying awake under the onslaught of pain and the terrible feeling that my blood was going to freeze solid in my veins.

I felt warm hands pressing me backwards and I let Milly lie me down, holding on to the realness of her like a lifeboat in my mind.

The pain eased a little now that I didn't have to stay upright, becoming waves rather than raw throbs. My breathing eased, so it rose and fell with the waves; the room was pulsing around me, as though I was lying on the surface of the sea, and for a wild moment I almost laughed as somewhere inside I thanked God it was going up and down rather than around and around like last night – at least I didn't feel sick.

SIXTEEN

There was nothing but darkness all around me, and I wondered what had happened. For a second I thought I might have died, and though the thought didn't scare me much, it didn't seem true either. No, this was familiar, I told myself. I'd been here before. I just had to remember.

With that, a faint light dawned all around me, so faint that I could just see the outline of my hand in front of my face. The blackness became greyness, and I peered into it. Then I realised it was snowing; the greyness all around me was snow, and the grey, impenetrable wall ahead of me was falling snowflakes, thicker than the heaviest snowstorm I'd ever seen.

I stood and stared for a moment, wondering how I'd gotten there. I tried to remember – I had been in my room with Milly. We were looking at Grandma's journal, trying to find something important. I felt a tingle down my spine as I realised I was dreaming again and I laughed. When Grandma had talked about going back to the forest of her homeland, she meant like this, in a dream. I stared around me in awe; I was really here. A laugh broke from me, falling flat in the swirling snow. This was real magic!

But where was here? I couldn't see any trees around me, even through the snow. In fact, I seemed to be standing in a wide open space; I could feel a great expanse of air around me as though I was standing in a field. There was no sound of tree branches in the wind, no shadows thrown by trees in the moonlight. Just snow, grey and swirling; soft like feathers in every direction.

I frowned. This wasn't like before. Something had changed. Something was wrong.

With that realisation came sudden sensation – I was cold. My bare feet stood deep in the snow, and the cold bit into them like teeth. A drawing ache crept up my legs and beneath my hair, the back of my neck was wet and raw with melted snow. I reached up to brush the flakes from my face, my fingers already almost numb at the tips.

It was so real; it wasn't like any dream I'd ever had. My teeth chattered and I clenched my jaw shut. And deep in the pit of my stomach, something more than the coldness of snow twisted like oil.

But where was I? The question was more urgent now. The greyness around me hadn't become any fainter; there was still nothing to see but snow.

Slowly, like a fingertip, fear slid up my spine and my whole body tensed. Something, somewhere, was watching me. Something was here with me, in the blank, grey emptiness. I hugged myself, trying to rub some warmth into my chest, and closed my eyes. Maybe if I just tried to, I could wake up and be back in my room with Milly again. But nothing happened. I was still as solidly and physically there as if my body was really in the middle of a snowy plain. I opened my eyes again, terrified that there would be something right in front of my face. There was nothing there.

Nothing but snow and more snow. I stood for a moment longer, shivering and watching as I grew more and more cold. If I stood there I'd just get weaker and more afraid. I had to do something. I had to move.

It was hard, but I urged myself to take a step, ignoring the gnawing fear that there would be nothing to stand on when I did. But there was definitely ground beneath my feet; I could feel it, solid and uneven beneath the crunching snow.

The next step was easier. I exhaled and watched my breath mix with the falling snow, then forced myself forward. I didn't know if I was going in the right direction, I only knew I had to move. I hoped Grandma was watching me, that she could help me.

The memory of her warm presence beside the fire gave me strength. I walked faster, more confident with each step. Behind me, I could feel the dark silence of the snow closing in, still and watchful. I didn't look back. Instead, I held onto that memory of firelight and I let it encourage me.

The snow cracked beneath my feet. I crept onward. I didn't know how long I'd been dreaming; it seemed that I'd been there forever in a world of dark, cold nothingness. But then, like a whale rushing upwards out of the deep, the forest was ahead of me. Trees loomed like silent watchmen, darker than the falling snow, but comfortingly solid.

I gasped with relief as I passed the first one and touched my palm to its bark. It was slightly warm; I could feel the life beating within, and it gave me strength to keep moving. But even as I passed underneath the snow-heavy branches, I felt something moving behind me, something almost as silent as the snow.

I swallowed my heart as it tried to climb up my throat, then forced myself to take another step. Behind me, the snow creaked in an echo of my footfall. Suddenly, I found myself in a sickening chase with the air ragged and freezing in my lungs and my feet stumbling over tree roots and slipping on patches of trampled snow. Always there were the steady, subtle, sounds of my pursuer, gaining ground.

I was too cold to run. My feet were numb and I could barely keep myself from stumbling. All I could think was that somewhere in this forest was a fire beside a cave, and there I'd find help. I held on to that thought as the panic caught at my breath.

My fear was like a scream rattling through my whole body. I knew it was the shadow stalking me without even having to see it. There was nothing else that could make me feel like this; there was nothing that could pull me into such a terrible dream as this. It was stalking me like a wolf, quiet and patient, because it knew there was nothing I could do against it. I hadn't managed to find the answer in Grandma's journal, and now I was on my own. Somehow, I knew, that if I let it catch me, I would never wake up again.

My tears froze on my cheeks as I thought about never going back to Mum, or to Milly, or to our spot in the woods. What would they think had happened? I wondered, then I forced myself not to think about it. I had to keep going; I had to find the help I knew was here, if I only knew where to look. Somewhere, Milly was with me –the real me –and she was trying to help. I knew that too. But I couldn't hear her. I was alone.

My blood stopped as my heart froze beneath my ribs. To my left, something huge moved against the background of grey. My legs gave up and I fell to my knees. Then the dark shape was gone and with a gasp of desperation, I stumbled back to my feet and tried to run, slipping on the ice and mud. It was loud behind me now, breathing heavily. My heart pounded into action again, all thought of the cold vanishing.

But then I heard another sound, like the cracking of branches, and I felt the cold pressure of the shadow, not from the left but from the right now. That meant there must be two of them, both hunting me between the trees. I sobbed, forcing myself to go faster, but I knew I'd never gain enough ground.

Somewhere in the snow I heard a snarl. I ignored it; it was all I could do to keep moving. I stumbled onward. Then I saw a light up head and staggered towards it. I didn't know if it was safety, or more danger. I didn't even know if it was real – if anything was real anymore. My chest felt like it was going to split open as I collapsed onto the ground, just within the circle of firelight.

SEVENTEEN

I wondered if I was dead for the second time, but beneath my face was hard, bare earth. I breathed in its cool, soothing scent and pressed my forehead to the ground. If I was about to die, I didn't want to see. I was too tired to fight or run; I just wanted to disappear and not feel anything anymore.

"Anne?" someone said. I shook my head, screwing up my eyes. I didn't want to move or think. But something was moving close to me, and the sliver of life I had left, the last bit of warmth and courage, rebelled against just lying there. Without wanting to, I curled into a crouch and looked up into the firelight.

There was a squat silhouette by the fire. As I blinked, it resolved into a figure, reaching out to me with a pale hand. I peered at it, then glanced behind me. There was nothing there. Just a wall of darkness; no trees, no snow. It seemed as though all that was left in the world was this campfire and the two of us sitting there.

I turned back to the fire and sat up straighter. My frozen toes were beginning to ache as the heat reached them, and my fingers cramped as I pushed my wet hair from my face.

"Anne," the voice said again. It was very calm and gentle, husky like soft, dry tree bark. I wiped my eyes with the back of my hand and squinted into the bright firelight.

It was hard to make out in the fluid shadows from the fire, but I slowly understood what I was seeing. An old woman was sitting on the ground, wrapped in a thick blanket lined with fur. Her hair was a deep, thick grey, and it cast a shadow over her face. She had turned from the fire to watch me, but she was sitting very still, her hand hanging in the air between us.

I looked around again, then stared back at her. I felt like one of the rabbits I sometimes saw frozen in the dusk light as I walked home through the woods. Deep in the shadows of her face, there was a shimmer of reflection – eyes watching me.

I watched her too, wondering what I was meant to do; this was the place I'd been trying to reach. It was the place I'd been looking for in all my dreams. Hers was the voice that had called me onward.

"Are you my Grandma?" I whispered, barely daring to break the silence. "Constance Orr?"

"Astrid," she said, making me jump again. "My name is Astrid."

She reached up and pulled her hair back, letting the golden light fall across her face. She was old, but not as old as I expected. Her eyes were dark, still in shadow, but they almost shone with life. The hand that reached to me curled its fingers, beckoning me forward. I swallowed, then edged a little closer.

The fire leapt and settled again. I flinched, glancing behind me to where the forest should have been, but there was only darkness back there. I shivered and forced myself to turn away.

Stretching my aching hands to the fire, I kept my eyes fixed on the old woman in case she moved. But she didn't; she seemed to know how scared I was and sat very still, letting her outstretched hand fall back into her lap as she looked at me.

I didn't move for a long time. The fear that had choked me slowly faded, as though it was being melted by the fire and dripping off me into the earth. I took deep breaths of the warm, smoky air and let my body unclench without thinking anything at all. And Grandma waited for me, as patient as a carved stone.

"Why am I here?" My voice cracked as I spoke.

Grandma shifted, staring into the fire. "Where to begin..." she said, and her voice sounded so far away. "You know you are dreaming?" she asked, glancing at me, and I realised her voice had a slight accent to it, like a melody beneath the words. I nodded at her, wrapping my arms around my legs and waiting for her to continue. She turned back to the fire.

"This is the dream forest," she went on. "The place my people – our people – come to when we die."

I swallowed. "Then...I'm dead?"

She threw back her head and laughed. "No, my love," she said. "No, you're only dreaming. A special kind of dream, but just a dream."

"I don't understand," I said, looking around. I had known from the beginning that it was a dream, but it was so real; it was hard to believe it.

Grandma sighed. "So much has been lost," she said. "So many treasures buried..." She glanced at me again, then broken into a wide smile. "But not forever."

I stared at her. The firelight was dancing across her face, making her features fluid and hard to see. I knew that I should be suspicious, cautious, but for the first time since the dream had begun, I felt safe and warm. I knew this woman, my bones told me. I could trust her.

Her smile widened. "You feel it," she said. "You and your

cousin. I knew you would."

"Feel what? What's going on?" I knew I couldn't stay asleep forever, and sense of time was coming back to me now. "Why am I here?" I gestured to the fire and the darkness behind me. "And what was chasing me?"

"I'll answer your questions," she said. But now her voice was coming from far away.

The fire was dimmer, its warmth fading. I tried to lean forward to hear what she was saying.

"Read the book," I heard, but then I couldn't understand what she said next. The shape of her was disintegrating as the dream fell apart

"Wait!" I tried to hold on, but it was too late. The darkness was like a tide coming in, and I knew that I was going back to my body; I was waking up. The fire vanished, there was a moment of pure blackness, and then my room swam in front of me to be replaced by a blurred face only inches from my own. I swore.

"Oh thank God," Milly's said, and there was a huge sigh. Her hands were still holding my shoulders. I could feel where her nails had been digging into me through my clothes, and I was lying on my bed.

"I thought I was going to have to call for your Mum," Milly said, backing away to give me room to sit up. I rubbed my face, blinked to clear my eyes, and felt the trace of drying tears running down the side of my face. I shielded my eyes from the glare of sunlight and squinted at her.

"Sorry," I said, grimacing. Had I cried, or shouted? I wondered.

Milly gave me a thin smile. "Are you all right?" she said.

I nodded, and my head throbbed a little as I did. "Yeah, just a bit woozy. How long was I out?"

"Almost a minute," she said, and I had to force myself not to laugh. It had felt like hours and hours in the dream; I couldn't believe it could have only been one minute.

Milly gave me a look. "It's not funny," she said, getting up off the bed. "I was really worried. I thought you were going to die or something. You looked so ill!"

I stifled my laughter and forced myself to look guilty. "I'm really, really sorry," I said. "I tried not to – I couldn't help it."

I waited for her to speak. We looked at each other for a few moments, and then she laughed as well.

"So..." she said, sitting down again. "What happened?"

I put my hands over my face and groaned. "Oh my God, you have no idea!"

EIGHTEEN

It took me the better part of an hour to tell Milly what I'd seen during the dream. She sat and stared at me, saying nothing until I'd finished, then shook her head.

"I can't believe all that happened in only one minute," she said. "It's unbelievable."

"I know – that's why I laughed. It's so weird to have just been there, and now be back here. This feels like the dream instead."

We stared at each other, and for the first time it hit me: this was going to change everything. Forever.

Milly ran a hand across her eyes and laughed. There was a shake in her voice. I wondered if she was realising the same thing as me, because she glanced with wide eyes at Grandma's journal, lying innocently where it had fallen off the bed. I reached out and took her hand.

"I know it's crazy," I said, "but it's also real. You know that, don't you?"

She turned back to me and nodded. "I saw something too, when you were gone."

The colour of her face changed as she said it, turning sickly pale. She caught my eye, then looked away.

"It was just as you lost consciousness," she said, "just after I laid you down – I thought I saw..."

I squeezed her hand. "It's okay," I said, blinking back tears. "I think I know what you saw."

I didn't want her to have to talk about it, but Milly shook her head. "It was leaning over you, all withered like a spider or a dead tree..." she said, tears spilling from her eyes, "but it was a person – or it had a head and hands and arms at least."

Neither of us spoke. I thought I felt, just for a second, a chill go through the room.

"It was horrible. Awful," she said. Then she covered her face with both hands and sobbed.

I took a deep breath then let it out very slowly. "It's okay," I said, pulling her towards me and hugging her tightly. "It's going to be all right."

She nodded against my shoulder. It was rare for Milly to get upset, and the sight of it made me feel even worse about what was going on. I squeezed her just like she'd hugged me earlier, and then I realised that I felt different than before; stronger and more certain.

"I know what I need to do," I told her.

She pulled away and wiped her face. "Read the book," she said, and I nodded.

"I'll leave it here with you."

"Thanks."

We both stared down at the journal. I wondered what Grandma had told me to read in there and how it would help me figure all of this out. I felt years older than I had that morning, as though the day had lasted for weeks and weeks.

"I was going to show you that page, remember?" said Milly. "Right before you passed out."

I stared at her for a moment; it felt like a lifetime ago. "Do you remember where it was?"

She nodded, stooping to pick up the journal and open it again. Then she glanced at me with an odd look on her face. "Just don't pass out again, okay?"

I snorted and shook my head, but I thought I felt, like an echo, a shiver of cold go through me; something stirring in the corner of my eye.

Milly held out the book and I opened it in my lap so we could both read. Forcing myself to ignore the uneasy feeling in my stomach, I turned to the page she was pointing to and began to read as quickly as I could, just in case I was interrupted again.

"Mother doesn't understand," the writing on the page began, "and I don't blame her – I can hardly understand it myself. But I know this does happen, and it's happened like this for thousands of years.

Grandmother says the same thing happened to her when she was my age. She told me a story about her Grandmother taking her into the forest when it happened, to tell her what she had to do. She said there were others as well – other children – that it happened to, always the same way. I just wish it hadn't happened to me."

I looked up at Milly and raised my eyebrows, but she just nodded and waved for me to keep reading.

"At least Mother doesn't still think that I'm doing it on purpose," Grandma went on. "She knows now that I can't help it, and that it's a good thing. At least, that's what Grandmother says. I'm not sure I believe her – it's way too strange and scary to be good.

But at least now I know that I'm not on my own, and I can do something about it. With all the strange noises and dreams

I've been having, I was starting to wonder if I was going crazy, but now I know that I'm not. I'm just not happy about what Grandmother says I've got to do."

I stopped reading and turned to Milly. "So she heard noises and had strange dreams too," I said. My hands were shaking as they held the book; this was something other people experienced. That made me a feel a lot better about it all.

Milly nodded, pulling her eyes away from the journal to look at me. "And her Grandmother knew about it, as well as other people back then," she said. "They knew what to do about it."

"Keep reading." She turned the page for me. "What happens next?"

The entry continued on the next page.

"Last night was amazing and terrifying. I had a dream, one of those strange dreams I've written about, and Grandmother was in it. But there was something else there too, something frightening. I could hear it behind the trees and I could feel it watching me. I forgot I was dreaming and thought it was going to eat me.

And when I woke up, Grandmother was in my room. She didn't say anything, but she took me out into the night without waking Mother up, and lead me into the woods. She took me to a place I'd never been before, and told me more than she's ever told me.

She told me stories at first, the old stories about how Tierne found our people and how we came to live in the forest. Then she told me how she became a dreamer, and how she meets with Tierne in the forest in her dreams, and how he teaches her. And then she told me how she'd conquered her fears, in the darkness of the forest, with the help of Tierne."

I swallowed the lump that had risen in my throat. "Something frightening, watching her in the forest," I said. "And her

Grandmother in the forest with this Tierne, conquering her fears – I wonder if that's the same thing?"

"It'll say," Milly said, gesturing to the book. Everything I needed was in this journal, I thought. Grandma had made sure of that. But just as I was turning back to read the next bit, Mum's voice came up the stairs.

"Milly!" she called, making us both jump. We looked at each other, and my stomach lurched.

"Milly," she called again, and I heard her footsteps on the stairs. I shoved the journal beneath my bed covers and Milly leaped across the room to the door. She glanced over her shoulder to make sure I'd hidden the book, then pulled the door open. My mum was just reaching the landing.

"Your mum's on the phone," she said, holding our phone out to Milly, who took it and held it to her ear.

I couldn't hear my aunt's voice, but Milly's frown told me I wasn't going to like the outcome of this call. She stood listening to the phone for a minute, then nodded and said "okay" very quietly. I sighed, thinking that her mum must need her for something as I cursed our bad luck. Milly hung up and put the phone gently on my desk, then turned to look at me, her face white.

A trickle of cold ran down my spine and pooled in my guts.

"What's wrong? Is she okay?" I leaned forward, ready to call my mum to drive Milly home. But Milly waved me back, collapsing on my chair and looking grave.

"It's not what you think – she's fine, at least. She's not ill," she told me. "But she knows we've got Grandma's journal."

I stared at her as the coldness in my stomach churned. I didn't know what to say.

"I've got to go home," she said at last, heaving herself to her feet.

"Can I still keep the journal?" I asked, keeping my fingers crossed.

Milly nodded. "I think you'd better, you need it and if Mum gets it back she's going to burn it. I just know it."

Her voice cracked at the thought and I put my hand over my mouth. I needed that journal, now more than ever.

Milly began gathering up her things and putting them back in her rucksack.

"I didn't do any homework," she said with a tight little smile, and my heart lurched at how tired and sad she looked.

I got up from the bed and wrapped my arms around her. "Don't worry," I said, "this whole thing has a mind of its own, remember? It wants us to know about it."

She took a step back and looked at me for a moment. "You're different," she said, and I nodded.

"I feel it."

We smiled at each other. Then we both sighed as she slung her bag onto her back.

"I'd better go," she said. "Wish me luck."

I wanted to ask what she was going to say to her mum, but it didn't feel like any of my business. I couldn't understand why Aunt Sandy had such a problem with us looking at the journal, and I didn't know what she would do if she knew I had it, but I trusted Milly to figure something out. My job was to look through as much of the journal as I could and find out what we needed to know.

We gave each other one last, grim, smile, and then Milly stepped out into the hallway. I watched her trudge down the stairs, listened to her tell my mum she had to go, and then heard the door shut behind her. I sank onto my bed, exhausted and confused. But I couldn't help being a little excited about the secret treasure I had hidden beside me.

"Hey," Mum said as she came up the stairs. "Is Milly okay? What did her mum say?"

I shrugged, leaning back on the bed and trying not to look at the bulge in the covers where the journal was hidden.

"I don't know," I said, wincing as I told the lie.

Mum nodded. "Dinner's in a bit," she said, turning to go back downstairs. "I'll call up – you stay there and have a nap or something. You look worn out from all that homework."

I tried to ignore the little squirm in my stomach at not telling her everything. It was awful to have to hide all this from her, but I just didn't know how she'd react. I sagged back onto the bed. Then again, Aunt Sandy might tell her anyway, and sooner rather than later.

My premonition came true: it was less than an hour later when I heard the phone ring again. Mum picked it up and I listened as she greeted Sandy on the other end. Pausing in the middle of the fascinating journal page I was reading, I was poised to hide Grandma's book as quickly as possible if I needed to. From what I could hear, Mum was trying to calm my aunt down so she could understand what she was saying. This, I told myself, was not going to be good.

Their conversation became a lot quieter as Mum withdrew into the kitchen and closed the door, probably, I realised, so I couldn't eavesdrop on her. I sighed and gathered up all of my notes and the journal and began wedging them behind my wardrobe, which was the best hiding space I could think of.

And it was a good job I did, because five minutes later Mum called up the stairs for me to come down. Her voice was not as cheerful as it had been only a little earlier. I grimaced and plodded down the steps into the kitchen where I found sitting at the table with the phone lying in front of her, her face set.

"Sit down please," she said, not looking directly at me. I sat down opposite her and wondered what Aunt Sandy had told her. I really hoped Milly was okay.

"That was your Aunt on the phone," Mum said, "as I'm sure you already know." I nodded, but it seemed my response wasn't required yet because she kept talking. "She's very upset. It seems that something important has gone missing from her house, and she believes that you and Milly have taken it."

She paused to shoot a sharp look at me, but didn't wait for me to speak before continuing.

"As you can imagine, I'm surprised, to say the least. And disappointed. I thought we'd had this conversation already."

I blinked at her, wondering what the hell she was talking about. Then I realised, and as she started to speak again, I interrupted her. "What did she say we took?"

Mum gave me a look so fierce that it made me wince. "She was too upset to tell me; she just wants to make sure you don't have it – I'm sure she believes, as I do, that if you had something you shouldn't you would want to make amends immediately."

I swallowed the rising panic in my throat, my mind racing. Aunt Sandy hadn't said what we'd taken; did that mean she didn't want my mum to know about the journal? I looked up into Mum's face and thought fast, wishing I knew what Milly had already told her mum.

Mum was staring at me, her face hard and her hands clamped together on the tabletop. She thought Sandy meant the ring, I realised with a thump of shock; no wonder she was so angry with me.

"Mum," I began, leaning forward and trying to prove to her with my eyes that I was telling the truth. "What you're thinking, it's not what Aunt Sandy's talking about."

She raised her eyebrows at me. "Oh really? And how can

you know what I'm thinking? Tell me that."

I sighed, rubbing my aching eyes. As I let my hand fall, I caught a flash of worry cross her face, but she covered it up. On top of all the other guilt and worry I was feeling, there was now a new layer of sadness that I was making her so worried about me after everything we'd been through.

"I'm really sorry you're so worried, and that Aunt Sandy's so upset," I tried again, thinking through every word. I took a deep breath, and said what I knew was going to open up a whole can of words. "But this isn't about the ring."

Mum looked at me, her face blank for a moment, then she shifted in her chair. "Oh really? Then what is it about?"

I sighed again; how on earth was I going to explain this? Mum was waiting for an answer and I wondered if she would believe the truth. Or would she cart me off to the doctor? I just didn't know if I could trust her, and that was the worst thing in the world. Anything would be better than having her look at me like that.

"It's not about the ring," I said again, weighing every word. "It's about something else – something that should be mine and Milly's anyway, but that Sandy hid it from us."

Mum's face went an even paler shade of grey, and she stared at me. "If you're trying to blame Sandy for you stealing something..." she began, but I interrupted her.

"I'm not," I said, shaking my head. She had to listen to me; I had to make her listen. "Honestly. Sandy didn't want me and Milly to have something that was left to us by our Grandma – Milly even saw the letter before Sandy burnt it."

It seemed as though the room span gently for a moment and I gripped the edge of the table as hard as I could. I could not pass out now, I told myself. Pull it together.

"I'm promise, Mum," I told her, my eyes welling with tears.

Mum stared at me for a long time. Neither of us spoke. The horrible sinking in my stomach had become a hollow pit; there was nothing more I could do if she wouldn't listen to me now.

"Can you prove this?"

Her voice was quiet. I looked into her face, a tiny wave of relief making it even harder to hold in the tears, and nodded.

"I can show you what it is she's talking about," I said.

Mum nodded once, and got to her feet. I closed my eyes for just a moment, hoping I was doing the right thing. Please, I thought, please Grandma, let this work out okay.

Mum followed me without another word, up the stairs and into my room. The light from the street was a soft golden grey. It lit up the floating motes of dust that swirled around us as I pulled the wardrobe away from the wall and slid out Grandma's journal.

Turning to Mum, I held it out. In the washed out light, it was the most colourful thing in the room. Mum frowned and took it from me. I sat on the edge of my bed to watch, keeping everything I could think of crossed.

She ran her hands expertly over the leather binding, feeling the markings of age and the softness of use. The sight of it sent a ripple through me, a mixture of cold nerves and anticipation, and I realised I was holding my breath.

Without looking at me again, Mum sat down in my chair, lay the book on my desk and gently opened it. I knew without even looking that she was reading my Grandma's name where it was written so beautifully on the first page. I waited for her to turn the page and begin to read.

But she didn't; instead, she gently shut the journal again and turned to me, her face strange. "This is what you took from Sandy?"

"Yes, well, I mean Milly took it from the attic, and we've

been looking at it," I said, trying to be as truthful as possible.

Mum nodded. "Well, I can certainly see that it's Grandma Orr's," she said, glancing at the book and then back to me. "Which would explain why Sandy was so keen to keep it from you both..."

She caught my eye, and I wondered how much she knew about what had happened between Grandma and Sandy and my dad. How much had they told her about why they'd fallen out?

"But that doesn't prove it was left to you," she finished, looking at me steadily. I nodded, swallowing.

"Grandma Orr wrote a letter to Milly, before she died," I said, my voice shaking. "It explained why she wanted us to have the journal. But Sandy found it and destroyed it, and hid the journal. Milly only just found it again the other week."

I had to force myself to keep breathing; my whole body felt like a violin string, thrumming with tension as I hoped beyond hope that she would understand. Silence spread over us like a thick blanket. The only sounds were the trees outside the window. I didn't dare to look at her anymore, so I just stared at the carpet.

Finally, I heard her stir. She was nodding. Her hand was resting on top of the journal, just lying there.

"Okay," she said, her voice breaking the silence and making my heart thump. "I believe you."

I looked up at her. "You do?"

"I do." She had a strange, half smile on her face. I stared at her, unable to speak as the tension that had been winding inside me began to flood out. It was going to be okay, I thought, sending up thanks to whoever had helped me out this time.

"But – why?" I asked.

She tilted her head a little. I wondered if I'd pushed my luck too far, but then she shrugged. "The most important question," she said, "is what are we going to do about this mess?"

I swallowed. "I need to keep the journal," I said, trying to stop my voice from betraying how desperate I was.

"I understand. But Sandy's really upset."

I clenched my teeth. "I don't want to be harsh," I said. "But I don't think she has the right to keep it from us. Not now. It's up to us if we want to know about our Grandma, isn't it?"

There was a pause, then Mum nodded. "Yes," she said, as thought she was thinking something through. "I do agree there – you're old enough to choose for yourselves. And I have to admit, I always did think it was a ridiculous argument..." she said, as though to herself.

I waited, holding my breath.

She looked back up at me with a grim smile. "You know Sandy and I have always got on," she said, and I nodded, my guts churning with nerves. "I don't want to upset her or hurt her, I respect her a lot, but I do believe she's wrong on this point. And that denying you girls this knowledge might do more harm than good – you deserve to know your heritage."

I swallowed again, forcing myself not to interrupt.

"So," she went on, ignoring my fidgeting. "I will back you up on this. You can keep the journal here, and I won't stop you from reading it."

I exhaled and a shiver ran through me. "Thanks, Mum."

She nodded, holding up a finger to stop me. I winced. "On the condition," she said, "that you share what you find out with me."

I relaxed again; I had expected something much worse than that.

"I've always been interested in your Grandma; I only met her a few times." She patted the journal beside her. "And I want to know you're not learning anything truly dangerous. Okay?"

I hesitated; how would we keep everything that had happened to me a secret if we were telling her what we knew about Grandma? On the other hand, maybe she wouldn't freak out about it all as much as I'd thought. She was being really cool about the journal right now, and that had to count for something. She might even be able to help us.

I looked her in the eye and nodded.

Mum beamed at me. "Great!" she said, getting to her feet. "Don't worry – I'll tell Sandy."

NINETEEN

"Is Sandy really angry, then?" I asked, sitting down to eat. I had been filling Mum in on some of the things I'd read in Grandma's journal; some of the less intense stuff.

She grinned at me over her plate. "She'll get over it," she said. "She must see the sense in letting you investigate."

Mum had called my aunt after we'd come down from my room and I'd heard most of their conversation as I cooked dinner for us. It hadn't sounded good, but thankfully, it had been a short conversation. I wondered what Sandy had told Milly.

"Do you think she'll let Milly come over tomorrow?"

"I don't know. She was pretty angry – you might have to give her some time," Mum said, catching my eye. "And I wouldn't encourage either of you to lie to her again either."

My face grew hot; I felt guilty enough about all the things I was keeping from Mum already without her pointing out my mistakes.

"Why are you so interested in Grandma Orr?" I said to change the subject.

"You know I love artifacts, old things, other cultures." Her eyes glinted as she spoke. "That's what I trained in, you know. I didn't always intend to be just a valuer."

I nodded; it made sense. Mum couldn't help bringing home old, sometimes broken objects and furniture from all over the world. On both times she'd gone traveling in the last few years, she'd brought back more artifacts than clothes.

"So you think Grandma was from another culture?" I asked, shoveling more food into my mouth.

"I know so. She came from somewhere in Northern Europe during the war, when she met and married your Granddad. But, from what I've heard, her people were part of some isolated group who were still living as they had for centuries, up in the snow."

I was listening hard. It all matched up with what I'd seen and read, which was reassuring. "You know," I said, watching for her reaction. "Milly says she was a witch."

Mum smiled. "Some people call it that, I suppose," she said. I could tell she loved talking about this. "It's a complex area with many nuances. Certainly in this country, people of that – shall we say belief – were often called witches. But in other cultures they have other names," she went on. "Like shaman, or healer, or elder."

"So they were like doctors?"

She shook her head, frowning a little. "No – not really. More like priests or storytellers... it's hard to explain."

I nodded. "They did those things – all of those things – but they weren't just those thing," I said, surprising myself with the words.

Mum looked surprised too. "'Exactly," she said, grinning at me. "That's it. They did many different jobs depending on where and when they were, but at the centre of what they did was a reverence for nature and the spiritual, which they seemed to see as the same thing. It's mysterious and fascinating."

"So where are they now?" I asked, too interested to keep eating.

"Oh, there are people who still practice those things, but they tend to keep to themselves – it's not like a club, or a religion you see. There aren't any authorities; it's much more individual than that."

That made perfect sense. I'd never seen much of a correlation between how I felt when I was out in the woods or looking at stars in the sky and what most of the priests I'd known had ever told me. Mum chuckled, breaking my train of thought.

"I actually did my thesis on this very subject – or part of it," she said. I shook my head, wondering why it had taken me so long to confide in her.

"It's wonderful to talk with you about it, and to find such a rich source of information about it from our own family," she said, grinning from ear to ear as though she might pop with delight.

"I'm really glad," I said, grinning too. "It's great to share it with you."

We beamed at each other in the soft evening light, and for the first time I felt like I had something deep and special to share with her. More than just being her daughter. We cared about something together.

"You know," she said, glancing at me out of the corner of her eye and trying to look casual, "some people say that this path, belief, ability, whatever it is – they say it's hereditary."

My breath caught in my throat.

"Your Grandma was supposed to be one of these people, a witch as Milly says. It may be she believed you and Milly had inherited her power or calling in some way, and that's why she sent you her journal."

I stared at her, feeling myself flush hot and pink again. How had she known?

"I..." I stammered, but Mum waved her hand.

"It's okay," she said. "You don't have to say anything; it's a lot to take in, I know. Think of it like a journey we're going on, a journey of discovery – every journey teaches you something about yourself."

I smiled at her, swallowing my nerves. Should I tell her what Milly had said about the letter, or would it be too much? For a moment, I saw myself sharing everything. Mum might even be able to get rid of the shadow for me, but then the vision faded. I just couldn't be sure yet.

I lowered my eyes and began to eat again. "So you think it's all real then?" I asked, trying to sound casual.

Mum hesitated. "I'm not sure. I believe there's something important in it, something many modern cultures have lost sight of, but I've never seen any 'magic' as such..." She laughed. "I can't believe we're talking about this! If your dad knew, he'd blow a gasket."

I laughed with her at the thought. "I don't understand why he and Aunt Sandy were so against it, why they hated it so much," I said as the laughter faded. "She was their mother, after all."

"Ah," Mum said, "but they were brought up in England, and their father thought it was all nonsense." She wrinkled her nose. "And I don't think they hate it – more that they fear it. It was so alien," she continued, "something that had the potential to make them alien. Do you understand what I'm saying?"

I thought about it; if it hadn't been for all the crazy stuff that had happened to me, would I have been so keen to believe that Grandma's strange beliefs had anything to do with me? Or would I have been more worried about what my friends would think about me if they knew? I couldn't be sure anymore.

"I think so," I said, giving her a tired smile. It had been a long day. Mum noticed instantly.

"Right," she said, getting up from the table and whisking away my empty plate. "You look exhausted, and I've kept you up talking for far too long. You need to get to bed."

I got up, happy but relieved to be excused from talking. "Thanks, Mum," I said, giving her a hug and trying to communicate all the gratitude and closeness I was feeling.

She hugged me back. "Thank you for trusting me," she said, then tilted her head, "eventually." I grimaced, but she just squeezed my shoulder. "Off to bed."

I headed upstairs, listening to the clatter of pans and the low rumble of the radio as I lifted my heavy feet one by one up the steps. I had never felt this tired before in my life. At least I knew now that it wasn't because of my new school.

The thought of how excited and nervous I'd been about school only a few short weeks ago made me smile. It felt like it had been a hundred years since then, and I was a completely different person. I hadn't worried about Emily and Holly not talking to me for days; it just didn't feel that important any more. I supposed it would be, when all this had calmed down, but for now I was quite happy not to worry about anything else.

Something was bugging me when I thought back over the last few weeks, but I couldn't put my finger on it. There was something I'd missed, I thought. Something important. What the hell was it?

I pushed open my bedroom door and trudged inside. My mind worked as I pulled off my clothes, trying to figure out what was missing. But I couldn't keep up the effort for long; I was just too tired. By the time I crawled into bed, I'd given up; it could wait, whatever it was.

I collapsed onto my pillow and pulled up the covers. Within moments of closing my eyes, I was fast asleep.

TWENTY

I didn't dream at all that night. In fact, I had the most restful, normal night's sleep I'd had in months. I woke up early, feeling clear and excited, and could hear Mum already singing away in the kitchen. I slid out of bed and stretched in the warm sunlight, grinning as I remembered yesterday evening.

I hated the thought of Milly being in trouble with her mum, and even of Aunt Sandy being upset with us, but Mum's fascinating insights were a huge consolation. The journal was sitting on my desk where she'd left it. It had a look about it that made me think it was pleased to be out in the open at last instead of hidden in the shadows. I smiled at it, brushing my fingers over the cover as I passed on my way to the door, then I frowned as the strange feeling of missing something came back to me.

It was still there – a niggle at the back of my mind – but I brushed it away. I had to get downstairs and talk to Mum before she left for work, and I'd have enough time to think about it later, on my own.

Opening the kitchen door, warm air and a delicious smell hit me and I groaned as my stomach woke up. Mum grinned as she handed me a plate stacked with pancakes and we sat down to eat together. She was clearly in a good mood, which I took as a good omen.

"You don't think it'd be a good idea to call Milly today, do you?" I asked, already knowing the answer.

"Er, no. I think that would be a terrible idea."

I propped my fork against my plate and sighed. "I know. It's just… I hate to think of her there on her own, in trouble. She might not even know I've still got the journal."

"She knows," Mum said, sipping her tea while she gazed at me over the cup's rim. She wasn't smiling, but her eyes had little creases at the corners that told me just how pleased she was.

"Really? How?"

"Because when I called last night to talk to Sandy, Milly picked up the phone," she said. "I told her what I was calling to say – we didn't get much time to talk, but she sounded happier when I'd told her. So she knows. Don't worry."

I blew out a long breath, shaking my head. "No wonder Sandy's annoyed with you," I said, wagging my finger at her.

She just shrugged. "Milly's nearly 16; she's going to be an adult soon," she said. "It's hard for us mums to accept, but we just have to get over it, to be blunt."

I looked at her, wondering if she felt like that about me.

"Anyway," she said, getting to her feet, "I've got to go. Sorry. You'll be okay today?"

"Of course," I said, grabbing the plates to take them to the sink. "I'll be fine."

"You know what I mean." She gently caught my wrist. "With what happened on Friday, I'm still worried about leaving you alone."

I felt a tinge of guilt and annoyance, but I understood why she felt like that. "I'll be fine," I told her as I looked in the eye.

"I promise – I'll call if I have any problems, anything at all."

She sighed and nodded. Then she leaned over and grabbed her purse from the table.

"Okay, I'm on the usual number, and I'll call to check in a few times…"

She hesitated, and I held my breath. I had already caused her enough trouble; I didn't want her to miss work as well. But she seemed to dismiss the worry. In a moment she had pulled on her coat, gathered up her bag and was at the door. We said a quick goodbye and she chided me back inside so I didn't get cold in my pyjamas. The next thing I heard was her car pulling away.

I turned back to the hallway with a deep breath. Once again, I was alone in the house. But now things were different. I steeled myself, then climbed back up the stairs to the bathroom.

It was surprisingly easy to push the memory of all the scary noises to the back of my mind, because after everything that had happened I still had loads of homework to do and I couldn't put it off any longer. I spent the next four hours hunched at my desk, writing essays and doing calculations as quickly as I could, stopping only to get a drink or look out the window at some of the last glorious weather of the year.

By lunchtime, I'd made enough progress to put off the rest of the work. I was itching to get back to Grandma's journal. With the house to myself and no interruptions this time, I thought I could read at least half of it before Mum got home.

Grabbing the plate of lunch that Mum had left me, I opened the back door and went to sit in the tiny patch of sunlight on our little lawn, clutching Grandma's journal under my arm. It was a truly beautiful day; the sky was cloudless and the soft breeze was warm rather than chilling. I stretched out my legs on the grass and closed my eyes, drinking in the feeling of being alone.

My stomach rumbled, reminding me of how hungry I was; those pancakes felt like a long time ago. I put the journal down in front of me and turned to pick up my plate, then paused. A long shadow slid across the garden, cutting out the sunlight. For a moment there was a brief gust of proper wind – not the gentle breeze of earlier – and I shivered. Then it passed. I looked up and the sky was clear again.

I began to eat my lunch, attempting to flick through the pages of the journal between mouthfuls. A lot of the book was so old that the pencil had faded to almost nothing, and I had to peer at it to make out any words at all. The breeze closed the pages every time I picked up my fork, so I kept losing my place. Finally, I gave up; it would just have to wait until I'd finished eating.

I pulled my jumper closer around my neck. The sunlight had faded again, leaving the garden dim with shadow. I swallowed my mouthful and looked up, then stared; the sky was just as clear and blue as it had been minutes earlier. My skin prickled as I glanced behind me at the living room door, then back at the journal.

How could I have missed it? I wondered, memory flooding back to me. I hadn't sat downstairs alone in weeks, had I? But I'd forgotten why in all the fuss over the journal. My spine was like a rod of ice in my back as I took a deep breath and tried not to look behind me again. There was something at the window, watching me. I could feel it as clearly as if was touching my skin.

I swallowed, my throat suddenly dry, and put down my plate as casually as I could. It had been in the living room that I'd last heard the strange voice, the one I had thought was just an imaginary friend. I almost laughed at myself for being so stupid – how could I have forgotten? Or was it something more sinister than that? I wondered, feeling sweat starting to cool on my face and arms. Had something been trying to distract me?

I pulled my thoughts away from my suspicions. What was I going to do? That was what I had to figure out. The garden was growing darker and darker all around me, while the breeze that had been so warm and pleasant was now whipping my hair against my eyes and making me shiver. Grandma's journal lay at my feet, the pages turning by themselves in the wind.

I looked down at it, trying to think through everything I'd read. Early in the book, Grandma had written about how she had confronted the spirit that had been stalking her – her fears in the forest, she'd called it – but she hadn't said anything specific about how. All she'd mentioned was Tierne, the strange man who had been her teacher, but how did that help me now?

I wracked my brains, hoping I'd read enough of the journal to know what to do. Grandma had told me I'd find all the answers there, in its pages, but I must have missed something. Or maybe I'd waited too long to read it?

The coldness grew all around me. I was almost shaking now, as I felt kisses of snow against my neck and stared around me to see where they had come from. Nothing stirred, either in the garden or in the house behind me. I sat as still as I could, trying to force my mind away from the horrible memory of the chase in the forest and the terrifying banging that had filled the house only a week ago. But it was as though a hole had opened up in my mind, and everything I didn't want to look at was pouring in; I couldn't shut it out anymore

I could hear Emily and Holly jeering at me, telling me how precious and self-absorbed I was. Then Milly was there, her face hurt and pale in my bedroom as I laughed at how long

I'd been asleep. Then my mum, tired and worried, yet again, and my dad, joking about having driven for an hour to see me in hospital, and then Aunt Sandy, crying down the phone in a panic to my mum, scared for me while I laughed at her and her fears. All this, and every other mean and selfish thing I'd ever done or thought whirled inside me like a storm.

I felt sick; I couldn't hide from it anymore, this terrible knowledge of how useless and hurtful I was; how much pain and worry I caused. It was my fault Dad had left – I had always known that. I had ruined my mum's happiness, and now I was doing it again.

I clutched at my head, moaning for it to stop. It seemed as though the world was spinning, dropping away beneath me again, but not from tiredness this time; instead, it was the pain in my heart, the terrible ache of guilt, doubt and reproach. I wasn't the right person to be doing this, I thought; I shouldn't be even looking at this journal – all I'd do was cause pain with it.

I gasped at the pressure growing inside me, blind to everything else. Tears blurred the garden, stinging in the howling wind. Behind me, I thought I heard, almost beyond hearing, a chuckle. Just one, and it turned my blood to ice.

I gasped again, trying to force myself to get a grip; this wasn't the moment to have a crisis of conscience, I told myself, but it was no use. The memories and the thoughts kept coming; they were a flood, drowning my mind until I felt like I was going to burst, disappear, or crack open.

My breath sobbed from my throat as I realised what I had to do; my way was clear. There was no place for me here – everyone in my life would be far better off without me, and then this pain, all of this trouble I had caused, would be over. It was the only way to end it.

For a moment, the thought of killing myself filled my mind until I could see and think of nothing else. Then that same spark of will and life, or maybe pure stubbornness, raised its head within me like a striking snake and I felt myself harden. I would not do that to myself. I knew it as clearly and surely as I knew that I was loved and that I loved; there may be horrible parts of me, I thought, but there were good parts too.

Immediately, the flood of memories and horrible words was a little further away. I took a huge breath, gripping the grass beneath me with numb fingers. As tears spilled from my eyes, my gaze fell on Grandma's journal. It lay rooted to the ground in front of me, barely stirring in the hurricane of wind that surrounded it.

Then I was picking up the book and pressing its pages to my face, whispering into it with all my strength.

"Grandma, Astrid, Tierne, please – help me...."

The world lurched, the wind became a roar in my ears, my whole body shook and seemed to fall a long, long way. Then I was standing in snow, surrounded by enormous trees as the echoes of a scream died around me.

TWENTY-ONE

Gulping at an unexpected mouthful of freezing air, I looked around. This was definitely the forest of my dreams, by daylight this time. Thick snow lay in banks between the pine trees and all I could see in every direction was white patched with rough brown. Alarming as it was to jump from one place to another with no warning, I was glad to be here. And I realised with a jolt that it had worked: I had asked for help, and something had happened. The thought made me glow inside.

The forest was bright this time, with sunlight streaming down between the tree trunks, making the snow glitter. For the first time, I realised how beautiful and peaceful it was here. It was certainly better than being alone in my house, I thought, shuddering at the memory of that heavy presence.

I wove my way through the trees, knowing that somewhere within them was what I needed. Up ahead, I would find my Grandma, and she would tell me what I needed to know. Certainty burned in my chest, keeping me warm even though I was bare footed again – but the gnawing cold of my last dream had vanished along with the darkness and fear.

I had no idea how long I walked. Time had no meaning there at all. The ground beneath me became steeper until I realised I was going uphill. The trees were spread out a little more there, opening to a wide clearing at the top of the mound that looked out over a broad, blindingly white landscape. I stood in the sunshine and stared, taking it all in and wondering what I should do next.

Then I heard a noise behind me in the forest, a mixture of a breath and a shuffle. I turned around to greet Grandma, raising a hand to wave to her, but my hand froze in mid-air. Standing between the trees, staring at me with great, black eyes and puffing hot clouds into the cold shadows, was the biggest, most rough and wild looking bear I had ever seen.

All thought of this being in a dream vanished; my body lurched away, skidding down the other side of the hill. The bear took a step towards me as I slid, and then it reared up, pawing the air and making the ground shake with its bellow. I choked as a cold nausea pressed into my chest, knowing this was it; another trap set by whatever was hunting me. It had lured me here, tricked me into this world and lulled me into carelessness with sunshine and beauty only to set upon me in the form of this great beast.

I screamed a long wordless scream of despair and turned to run. I wouldn't let it do this. I had no power, no clue what I was doing, but I'd be damned before I just lay down and let it do what it liked to me. My feet pounded in the hard snow, slipping with every step as I half-ran, half-slid down the slope towards the trees on my left. Behind me, I could hear the rasping breath of the bear as it bounded after me.

We ran, ducking through the trees as they grew thicker and thicker again. I didn't know where I was going or what I was going to do; I just knew I had to keep going. My breath seared my lungs and throat and exhaustion was beginning. After everything I'd gone through in the garden earlier, and now this, I didn't know how much longer I could keep on. My eyes burned as though I was going to cry, but no tears came. The air stung my face and the low branches whipped my hair and clung to my clothes, holding me back.

It didn't make any sense. I tried to work out what had gone wrong as I stumbled forwards, but it was too much work just keeping upright. Behind me, I could hear the bear growing louder with every step and I knew it was gaining on me. My heart screamed at the unfairness of it, but I forced myself onward until I slipped again and sprawled head first into the snow.

It was all over; there was nothing more I could do. In a breath, the great bear was standing over me, its wet muzzle billowing air as it looked down at me with dark, alien eyes, and my chest throbbed as I clung to life.

But the bear didn't move; it stood above me as I lay motionless, too tired to fight, and looked down at me steadily, silently. My heartbeat was so strong that I could feel it in my hands and neck; surely the bear could hear it, smell my blood. It would soon take me in those huge jaws. But nothing happened.

It watched me as though waiting for something. For a long, long time, neither of us moved; the forest around us had settled to silence again, the sunlight streaming down in ribbons of gold that glittered like jewels on the snow. My heartbeat slowed. I swallowed the lump in my throat as I began to think again.

What had I missed? What hadn't I understood? Was there something in Grandma's journal that explained what was happening now? I edged my hands up to my face and wiped the melting snow out of my eyes.

I looked up into the bear's face again, only inches away from my own. His fur was thick with a dusting of snow that looked like patches of icing sugar, and his eyes were bright and alive. But he was old, too. There were great scars beneath the fur on his shoulders and his throat rippled as he breathed; his snout was scarred as well. He stood and let me look at him, not moving even a single claw, and I realised I was going to have do something.

I propped myself up on my elbows a little. "This is a ridiculous."

It was the first thing that came to my mind and it was how I was feeling, but I winced as soon as I said it. But I only had to worry for a moment, because then the great jaws opened and the trees all around us were ringing with laughter; the bear was laughing at me.

I wrinkled my nose at his wild, earthy breath and huffed.

"Well, it is," I said.

"Yes," he said, in a voice like thunder and storm winds through treetops. "You have at least got that right."

I stared at him, my eyes as wide as they would go. A bear had just spoken to me. But staring didn't change what I was seeing, so I closed my eyes for a moment, wondering if when I opened them he'd still be there. He was. And now it seemed as though his eyes were smiling as he looked down at me on the snow.

I huffed again and sat up straighter, backing away so I had room to look at him properly. And what, I thought, am I supposed to say back? The thought was like a dam bursting inside me, and I found myself laughing, holding my hand to my mouth to muffle the noise. The bear laughed again, shaking snow off the nearest branches.

It took me a few minutes to calm down; after all the fear off the last who knew how long, I felt like a too tightly wound spring. After all the tension had poured out of me in a mixture of laughter and tears, I wiped my face and looked up at the bear again. He hadn't moved an inch.

"Who are you?" I asked.

"Tierne."

"Ah."

Now it made sense; I had assumed that Tierne was a man, someone who had taught my Grandma, but he didn't need to be. Clearly, he was something else entirely.

"You're a bear," I said, feeling stupid but wanting to be completely clear.

His eyes sparkled like the snow, and he nodded. I thought for a moment before continuing.

"You knew my Grandma," I said, and he nodded again.

"Yes, I know her. She asked me to come to you," he said, shifting his huge paws in the snow and then settling himself down onto his belly so he was almost the same height as me.

I swallowed; seeing him move, close up, was intimidating. "Why?"

He looked at me out of the corner of his eye, but didn't answer my question. Instead, he said, "You don't know much, do you?"

That stung; I had thought I'd been doing pretty good, considering I had no one to teach me. Apparently I was wrong. He laughed again, making me wince.

"It's all right, little cub," he said. "You have a long time to learn."

I leaned back against the tree behind me.

"So why did Grandma send you to me?" I asked. "Why didn't she come herself?"

He nodded, sighing a little and settling himself even more. "Your Grandma is dead," he said. I nodded and he went on. "So, for her to come and talk to you is... complicated. This is where I live, and this is what I do – it's easier for me."

I thought about this, wondering if it made any sense. "Okay," I said, "so why did you come then?"

Tierne paused for a moment, and I wondered if he would avoid the question again.

"Because you need some help, and because you are... family," he said at last, staring at me in a way I couldn't figure out. I opened my mouth to ask another question, but he raised his paw and spoke again. "I would like to answer all your questions," he said as gently as giant bear could, "but we don't have much longer – you have to return soon."

I felt a flicker of fear in my guts at the thought and he nodded.

"You do need my help," he said, "and I will give it. But first, you must do something."

I frowned at him, suspicious. "What?"

"You must make your choice," he said.

I shivered. A hush had fallen all around us. "I have no idea what that means."

A tremor ran through the ground beneath me. I leaned forward and pressed my hands into the snow. Not yet, I thought. I don't know what to do yet. But around Tierne, shadows deepened.

"Read the first pages of your Grandmother's journal again." His voice rang in my mind as my vision darkened.

"But what about the shadow...?"

It was too late; I heard his voice again, too faintly to understand, and then I was surrounded by blackness. I spun and tumbled in the air for a moment, then I was lying flat on my back in the warm September sunlight with a clear blue sky above me, a gentle breeze rippling through the pages of Grandma's journal.

TWENTY-TWO

I pushed myself up off the grass and then sat with my head in my hands as tears seeped from beneath my eyelids and I brushed them away. This was not the time to get weepy, I told myself. I had something important to do.

A glance at my watch told me that barely five minutes had passed since I'd sat down for lunch; I couldn't believe it. Had it all really happened? It seemed like a story from someone else's life. I was so normal – or I had been until all of this happened.

A silent wish rose inside me that I'd never heard of the journal at all, and I smiled at myself. It seemed ridiculous to think like that now; my life was changed and there was no going back.

And I wouldn't have chosen otherwise, I realised with shock. Thinking this made me feel stronger, as though my heart had set into steal. I thought back to what Mum said at breakfast, that parents find it hard when their children grew up. I was doing just that – growing up. Everything I looked at was changing before my eyes, growing bigger and stranger and more complicated. I sighed and got to my feet, grabbing the half-empty plate and Grandma's journal.

Inside, the house was cold but I didn't let myself think about it. I ducked into the kitchen, ditched my plate and headed for the stairs. All I could think about was getting up to my room and reading the pages Tierne had told me to find. That was my only choice; there was no other solution.

The phone rang as I passed it. I hesitated; did I want to talk to anyone right now? What if it was Mum checking up on me, she'd worry if I didn't pick up. I lifted it to my ear.

"Hello?"

"Anne, thank God," said a small voice on the other end of the line. I smiled.

"Milly, are you all right?"

There was a low chuckle before she answered. "Yeah, though I think I might be going deaf from all the yelling. Mum was furious."

I winced. It was awful to think of them fighting so badly. "Is she okay now?"

"No, and she won't be for ages, but don't worry about it. We're right, and your mum agrees with us. Grandma's journal was left for us and we're old enough now to read it. And besides, you need it."

She was right, but that didn't make me feel any better.

"Anyway," she went on, "Mum's gone out with the boys. I'm supposed to stay here and study, but she'll be out for hours – shall I come 'round?"

I grinned despite myself. She was the most determined person I knew. "If you think it'll be okay."

"It will. Don't worry about it. Toady does bad stuff all the time and she's okay with him."

I laughed; she was right about that. "When can you get here?"

"Give me half an hour. I've got to get some stuff," she said, then put the phone down.

I grinned. Just talking to Milly made me feel more normal than I had all day. It would be great to see her and tell her everything that had happened.

My room was much warmer than the living room. I clicked the door shut behind me and curled up in bed with Grandma's journal. Outside, the sky was still clear and sunny, and light was flooding the whole room. It made me feel safe, sitting in its warmth, and I decided to stay there until Milly turned up. I stuffed my earphones into my ears, turned on some music and began to read.

"I went into the forest with Grandmother tonight. We had a fire in the snow and sang and played drums and told stories, and then I made my choice, right there with everyone watching. It was just how I'd imagined it should be, and I felt so proud today, seeing how everyone looked at me differently. Even Mother was different, even thought I could tell she was sad about it too."

I found the right page with my first try, it seemed. I read on, searching for more clues.

"Now my real work begins, I suppose. Before I've just been learning basic stuff – the stories, what the work is for. Now Grandmother says she can begin to teach me the practices and things, and we can start to figure out what my power is. It means I can begin going to the ceremonies with her."

This made a bit more sense; it sounded like some kind of initiation, I thought. I would have to ask Mum when she got home – this was exactly the kind of stuff she'd know about. A tingle of frustration ran through me as I wished Grandma had explained more in her journal, but I already knew why she hadn't. My aunt had it for ages – years – and who knows who else could have gotten a hold of it if Milly hadn't found it.

Grandma hadn't wanted to share all her secrets with just any old person. I smiled at that thought, proud. Even though I hadn't ever met her, I felt more connected with my Grandma now than almost anyone else I knew – it was like we were a real family, somehow.

I turned back to the journal, aware that Milly would be arriving soon and wanting to get as much information as possible before she did. But I couldn't see anything else that was helpful. I flicked back a page, seeing if she'd written anything about this choice before that night, but I couldn't find anything.

I sighed and put the journal down beside me. This was just another mystery, I thought, rolling my eyes. Was this the best Tierne could give me? At the memory of that enormous presence, I shivered a little, feeling for just a sliver of a moment like I was back in the forest. Then it passed, and I shook my head, feeling reckless.

"What am I supposed to do now?" I asked just in case he could hear me.

No answer came. I didn't expect one; from reading the journal, I was beginning to understand more about how this worked – it wasn't like someone laid out stepping stones to follow or gave you a map. You had to find your own way, because your way was different to everybody else's; that was what made it so amazing and powerful.

Tierne had said I needed to make my choice; I supposed he meant that I needed to do whatever it was Grandma had done on that night so long ago. It sounded like a big thing too, something I would need to think about, but how on earth could I find out what it was or how to go about it? If there was nothing else in the journal about it, where could I find more information?

I looked at my computer. Surely, it would be far too secret

to be just lying around on the internet, I thought, but it was worth a try. I settled myself down in the chair and turned the screen on. It was 20 minutes since I'd spoken to Milly, and I had just enough time for a quick search before she arrived.

I typed in my question and hit enter, rolling my eyes at the idea that this would be anything more than a big waste of time. But I kept my fingers crossed, closed my eyes and hoped Grandma was helping. I scanned the headlines, not even sure if I was reading them. I felt odd, fuzzy headed, and I wondered if I should have eaten the rest of my lunch.

There was nothing on the screen that answered my question, but I couldn't bring myself to click on the next page. What was going on? I wondered as I felt even fuzzier. Then my head cleared and the page in front of me grew brighter. I blinked, trying not to freak out as the words swam and shuddered in the blank space of the browser; not moving, exactly, but some were getting bolder and bigger while others shrank and faded to almost nothing.

I blinked again, afraid to move and break whatever magic this was. The background behind the words was still white, but now there were thin lines, delicate like spider's silk, trailing between the bolder words and shining as if the sun was glinting on them.

I followed the trail as it lead between the words. It read, "Do you want to walk this path?" Just that. I stared, wondering if I was reading it right, and knowing I was.

"Is this you, Tierne?" I asked aloud, knowing the answer immediately. It wasn't him – it was my Grandma, showing me what I needed to know. As I silently thanked her, the words settled and the shining trail vanished, and then my head buzzed as though I'd stood up too fast.

Do I want to walk this path? I repeated to myself. So that

was the choice Tierne had meant, and it made sense. It was so simple; I was amazed that I hadn't figured it out for myself.

I got up from the computer and paced the room. Outside, the afternoon sunlight had faded, turning greyer and more blustery as the weather changed. I stared out of the window for a few moments and my heart ached. I had known for days that this was a big moment for me. The more I learnt about Grandma and her 'path', the more I could feel myself – my whole life – changing. But to be asked to choose, to commit to it with so little information? It seemed unfair, rushed.

There must be another way, I thought to myself, wondering if I'd get an answer to that question as well. Nothing came, and I didn't expect anything else. Milly would be here soon. At least I'd have lots to tell her, I thought with a tired chuckle.

TWENTY-THREE

The sky was just turning a hazy pink when Milly arrived, a little out of breath. I was waiting for her at the door, watching the clouds as they gathered to the East like mountains.

"Hi," Milly said, scrambling up the steps and giving me a quick hug. I let her pass, then shut the door behind her.

"How're you doing?" she asked, taking off her coat and giving me an intense look. I shrugged; what more could I say?

She gave me a grim smile. "Come on, let's get a cup of tea."

I followed her into the kitchen and flicked on the kettle. Milly leaned against the cabinets and folded her arms, watching the clouds that were rolling into view outside before turning back and smiling at me again.

"So," she began, setting out the mugs and pouring the hot water. "What's happened?"

I snorted. Now that it came to it, I didn't know if I wanted to tell her everything that had been going on. Milly eyed me over her cup and waited.

"First, tell me how it's been for you." I said, avoiding her gaze and taking a sip of tea.

She hesitated before answering. "It's been... okay," she said. "Mum's – well, we'll be all right."

I nodded, looking at her and waiting for the 'but'. Milly caught my eye and gave a cheerless laugh.

"But...?" I asked, encouraging her to continue.

She sighed. "But there's something else," she said. "Other things..."

She had gone pink despite the fact that the kitchen was growing cooler by the moment as the afternoon turned to evening. I raised my eyebrows. "Other things like what?"

"Like, it's hard to explain," she said. "What about you?"

I laughed; neither of us wanted to go first. "Okay," I said, putting down my cup. "Something happened this morning. It was pretty intense. I was in the garden, eating lunch, and I had Grandma's journal with me because I hadn't had any time to read it all morning – I'd been catching up on homework."

Milly nodded. "So what happened?"

I paused, wondering how to describe it. Just remembering what had happened was making me feel sick. "I felt it... more clearly than ever," I told her. "It was there, behind me in the house, looking out. And before I could do anything it... well, it..."

I hesitated. It sounded so crazy, there was no way she would believe me. I looked at her, at a loss for words. But Milly nodded.

"It spoke to you," she whispered.

I swallowed. "Kind of."

"Like in your head," she added, and I nodded, feeling my skin prickle.

"What did it say?" she asked, and I hesitated again; it was hard to confess to, even to my best friend.

"I thought about... how much worry and trouble I'd

caused," I said. My mouth was dry, making the words catch. "I remembered all the times I'd done something horrible, or mean, or selfish." I looked up at her and caught her eye. "It felt horrible. Awful."

She nodded, clutching her cup in front of her like a shield.

"But it wasn't a voice," I said. "Not like before – it was just my thoughts."

Milly frowned. "Like before?" she asked, and I realised I hadn't told her that part.

"I remembered something this morning, just before it happened," I told her, shifting in my chair and feeling my cheeks burn. "I spoke to it, weeks ago – all summer, really."

Milly's mouth fell open. "Why? Why would you do that?" she asked, and I shook my head.

"It wasn't like that. Not then," I tried to explain, grasping for the right words. "It was just a voice. There was no shadow, no noises, no coldness, nothing like that. It was just a voice."

It sounded pathetic, and I knew it; would she think I'd done this on purpose, or that I had wanted it to happen? I tried to explain again, knowing I'd have to say the thing I didn't want to confess.

"I, well… I thought it was just my imaginary friend, you know?" I said, the words sticking in my throat as I looked away from her. There was a moment of silence.

"Your imaginary friend?" she aksed. Her voice was quiet.

I nodded without looking at her. The silence stretched on again and I waited; Milly was my best friend in the world, I had to trust she wouldn't hate me or laugh at me, even now.

Finally, I realised I was going to have to look back at her. Turning, I saw she was staring out the window, her face pale but calm.

"Milly?" I asked, not wanting to disturb her.

She turned back to me and smiled, looking tired. Then she shook her head. "It's all so amazing. All of this..."

I frowned, not understanding. "You – you don't think I'm mental then, or really childish?"

She laughed and reached over to take my hand. "What? No," she said. "Did you really think I'd believe that?"

I swallowed, feeling my shoulders relax and letting myself smile back at her. "I don't understand, then."

Milly nodded. "You spoke to this shadow-thing over the summer because you thought it was your imaginary friend, right?" she asked, waiting for me to answer. I nodded but said nothing. "Because you had an imaginary friend a long time ago, I bet, when you were little?"

Again, I nodded.

Milly sighed.

"It's just strange," she said. "I had an imaginary friend too, when I was small."

"You did?" I asked, incredulous, and she smiled at me.

"Uhuh. And I thought it had come back this summer as well."

I stared at her, not knowing what to say. We looked at each other in silence for a moment, the shadows across our faces growing as the light dimmed outside.

"What happened?" I whispered.

"Huh?"

"I mean, why did you think it was back? What did it say?"

"It was just a voice, like you said," she told me, shaking her head. "But I didn't listen to it. I didn't want to listen. I ignored it completely."

I thought about it for a moment; this was too much of a coincidence to not be linked with the shadow.

"Why?" I said her.

She sat up straighter and looked at me. "Because... because I didn't want to be a little kid, I didn't want to think about imaginary friends and the time I had one."

I nodded. "So you didn't talk back to it?" I asked, and she shook her head, deflating again.

"No. And I only heard it maybe three times? No more than that."

"And then it went away?"

She nodded, catching my eye. "Do you think that's why this all happened to you, and not to me?"

"I spoke to it," I said. "I told it things for weeks. I let it in."

My cheeks burned again; this was all my fault, just like the shadow had said. If I hadn't been such a baby, none of this would have happened. I would still just be a normal girl.

But Milly shook her head and squeezed my hand in hers.

"It's not your fault; I understand why you spoke to it," she said. "I wanted to as well."

"You did?"

She nodded, but it didn't make me feel any better. "So you remembered this, and realised what had actually been happening," Milly said, pulling me out of my thoughts.

"Yeah, I remembered that I'd last spoken to it in the living room. I'd told it to go away and it had. But I hadn't wanted to go in there since – not on my own."

Milly nodded, thinking something through. "What did it want? Why did you tell it to go away?"

I rubbed my eyes, trying to remember. "It... it wanted to be friends with me. It didn't want to me to talk to anyone else, or to need anyone else. It told me no one understood me."

I gasped and stared up at Milly.

"What?"

"That was it – that was the conversation that made me ask

Emily about not being understood. It was the whole reason we argued." I couldn't believe I had forgotten.

"Ah. So you told it to go away," she said. "After talking to it for weeks, getting closer and closer. You shut the door, and then all the noises started."

I nodded into my hands. How could I have let this happen? And why had I forgotten it all?

"It's all right," Milly said. "This is great – we're getting somewhere."

I tried to laugh, but it came out as more of a huff. Milly laughed.

"Come on," she said, setting down her empty mug and getting to her feet. "Let's go upstairs. I suppose it's warmer in your bedroom?"

I nodded and followed her out of the kitchen.

It was warmer in the bedroom – just. The window was a bright blur of golds and roses and greys as the sun made its way down beneath the houses at the end of the street. Clouds towered and swelled just within sight, and the temperature had dropped so much that I wondered if it would snow tonight.

"It's gotten cold quickly, hasn't it?" Milly asked, rubbing her arms with her hands.

I dug out another jumper and pulled it on, then offered her a blanket.

"You didn't finish telling me what happened earlier," she said, wrapping it around her. "How did it end?"

I sat beside her on the bed and began to tell her the rest of the story, skipping as much as possible over the contents of those terrible thoughts and how desperate I'd become to end them. Instead, I focused on the chase through the forest and how the great, terrifying bear had turned out to be none other than Grandma's teacher, Tierne.

Milly laughed out loud when I told her, shaking her head at me. "No way," she said. "That's wonderful."

"It was amazing," I told her. "One minute I thought I was going to get eaten, the next I was being laughed at by a giant bear."

I felt lighter than I had all afternoon.

"So what did he tell you?" Milly asked, still giggling.

"He told me he'd help me," I said. She gave me a thumbs up, but I shook my head.

"It's not that easy though," I went on. "I have to 'make my choice' first."

"What does that mean?"

"Exactly," I said, recognising her reaction. "That's what I thought. He told me to read the first few pages of the journal, which I did."

"Did it help?"

"Not much."

We both chuckled again, and Milly leaned over to grab the journal from my desk.

"What did they say, the pages?"

I shrugged. "Read them; it won't take long," I told her, and she let the book fall open in her hands.

While she read, I looked out the window again. The sky was swirling with clouds now; they covered at least half of its washed out blue. I shivered, pulling my jumpers even closer around me and trying to check that nothing more than the weather was making me feel cold. But I couldn't feel anything unusual – no darkness at the edge of my vision, no movements in the shadows as I turned my head. I had become so used to the almost constant presence of the shadow that its complete absence was almost disturbing; I wondered where it had gone and why.

Milly closed the book and looked up at me, shaking her head. "Well, it's kind of useful," she said, looking out of the window as well. "It sounds like an initiation."

"That's what I thought."

"Exactly. But what does it involve, and what's it for? That's the question."

"Well, I haven't told you the last part yet," I said, and she turned back to me, raising her eyebrows.

I explained as clearly as I could what I had seen on the computer screen; how the words had become fluid and formed a chain, spelling a question: do you want to walk this path? Milly listened in silence, drinking in every word. When I finished, she grinned at me.

"Do you know what this means?" she asked.

"What?"

"It means you're a witch too," she said, her face glowing.

I frowned at her and shook my head.

"No, really, it does," she went on, ignoring the faces I was making. "You can do all of this stuff, you can dream like she did, and now you've actually scryed for something as well – without even trying."

"Scryed?" I asked, forgetting for a moment that I was trying to discourage her.

"It means... like seeing patterns and answers in unrelated things," she explained, waving her hands around. "Like people reading their futures in tea leaves, or tarot cards, but you actually did it for real."

I thought about it, unsure whether it was the same thing at all. What had happened had just, well, happened. It wasn't like I did anything. But Milly wasn't going to let me argue.

"You're a witch and Grandma knew it; that's why she sent us the journal."

"Yeah, but she sent it to you," I pointed out, "not to me."

Milly flapped her hands as though swatting flies. "That's just because you were too young to read then," she said as though I was being particularly stupid. "And I suppose she might have thought I could be one too."

I nodded, feeling uncomfortable. It did seem to make sense. There was no denying it. Even my mum had said these things could exist. My stomach churned and I tried to ignore it.

"But you've seen stuff too," I said, pointing at her.

She shrugged. "Not as much – nowhere near as much as you," she said, avoiding my eyes.

I squinted at her. "Hang on," I said, "you haven't told me what happened to you earlier."

Milly squirmed, not looking at me.

"Come on," I insisted. "I told you."

"Oh fine," she said, and I grinned. She ignored me. "Mum's been so cross with me that I've been spending almost all my time in my room since last night," she began. "Which is fine by me, because I had homework to do and lots to think about without her nagging me about the journal all the time."

I felt a pang of guilt at this change in their relationship.

"Anyway, it was last night before I went to bed," Milly went on. "Mum and Mikey were already asleep, and Toady was out. So I was practically on my own, with no interruptions. And I... well, it's like you said earlier," she said, hesitating and looking at me for my reaction. "Like you heard a voice, but just in your head."

I watched her, feeling more and more uncomfortable but not wanting to show it.

"I couldn't see anything, but I could feel it – that coldness I've felt around you when... well, you know. Like yesterday morning."

I nodded, sitting very still. Milly swallowed, still looking at me with a pale face.

"You don't think I'm making it up, do you?" she asked, and I almost laughed, but managed to hold it in.

"Making it up?" I shook my head at her. "After all I've seen, do you think wouldn't believe you? Don't be stupid!"

She laughed, but her voice was shaking. "Well, I just thought I'd check. That's it, really. I heard the thoughts – or voice, or whatever it was – and it was pretty bad, but then it stopped and I went to sleep."

"Why did it stop? What was it saying?" I asked, trying to understand.

"Not nice things," she said, sounding much younger than she was. The look on her face made me hesitate, and after my own brush with this particular phenomenon, I wasn't sure I wanted to know more than that. Some things shouldn't be repeated.

"But why did it stop?"

Milly shook her head and shrugged. "I don't know – it wasn't like I asked for help like you did or anything. I didn't need to; it didn't get that bad."

She caught my eye and I looked away; I never wanted to talk about how bad I'd felt this morning ever again.

"I just, well, I suppose I just told it to go away," she said, shrugging.

I thought about it; how was that different from what I'd done? Had I told it to stop, to go away? I realised with surprise that I hadn't. I had pretty much accepted that it was from inside me, in fact, rather than assuming that it was a 'voice' from outside that I could banish.

I stared at her.

"What? What is it?"

"Nothing." I held up a hand to try and stop her from panicking. "Nothing like that – it's just… I realised you did something I didn't."

"I did?" She looked stunned.

"Yeah. You told it to go away – I didn't think to do that at all."

We looked at each other. My mind was whirring frantically. What did this mean? I asked myself, but there was no answer. There were no more pieces for me to fit into this puzzle right now.

But there was one good thing about it, I realised.

"See," I said, giving Milly a look. "You are having stuff happen too – you're a witch if I'm one."

I didn't know why it made me feel better, but it did. The thought of being on my own in this was horrible, but the chance that Milly could understand, would go through it with me, was a huge relief. To my surprise, she didn't look upset.

"Yeah, I suppose you're right," she said. Then she grinned. "Wow."

I smiled back, glad I hadn't upset her.

"So what are we going to do?" She leaned forward and hugged Grandmother's journal to her chest.

"What do you mean?"

"About what Tierne said – the choice?"

"Oh," I said, my guts twisting again, "that."

Milly shook her head at me and waved the book around. "This is great," she said. "Why aren't you excited? We have the solution, or at least part of it – a step in the right direction."

I shrugged; I couldn't explain it to her, and I didn't know if she would understand even if I could.

Milly had always been different from other kids. Her mum was different – in a wheelchair a lot of the time – and that by itself had meant she did things and experienced things differently to other people. But it was more than that; much more. Milly's dad had died a long time ago, but not so long ago that she didn't remember; she had a different perspective because of that as well. And she was so full of life and confidence, so determined and strong; she was unlike anyone else I'd ever met.

But me – I was normal. I was used to being normal. My mum was pretty normal, and even my dad was normal, even if he was a bit of a skunk. I lived in a normal house and had normal friends and just, well, I had never been different. And I had liked that; it had been part of who I was.

But now, I was different. Really, really different. I had already seen what it had done to two of my friendships; I wasn't sure if I could handle that happening with anyone else. I liked having friends, going out, going shopping – what if being a witch, or whatever this was, meant I couldn't do those things anymore? What if this difference made me even lonelier?

I sighed, all of these thoughts running around my head, while Milly watched me with a shrewd look on her face.

"This is why it's so important," she said, pulling me out of my reverie.

"Huh?"

"This is why making this choice is so important," she repeated, leaning towards me. "Because we can't be half-in and half-out of it – we can't just mess about with it, but not commit."

I huffed at her, unwilling to admit she was right. I knew it was what needed to happen, I just wasn't sure I was ready.

"I don't understand why Tierne can't help me first," I said, knowing that I sounded whiny. "Why can't he just give me a bit more time before putting this pressure on me? Why does it have be now, when I'm under duress like this?"

Milly shrugged. "It makes sense to me," she said, then she froze and stared at me.

"What?" I asked, ready to get up and see the shadow behind me, but she waved for me to sit down and relax.

"No, don't worry," she said. "I just realised something."

I waited for her to continue, trying to settle the adrenalin that had just rushed through my body.

"I think I know why it has to be now. Actually, I think I know why this is happening like this, the noises and shadows and stuff... it makes total sense."

I raised my eyebrows. She shifted on her chair and wrinkled her nose for a moment.

"Okay, just let me get this right in my head first...."

I sighed and rolled my eyes and she gave me a look.

"I think this shadow-thing, whatever it is, is here now because you've got to make this choice."

I blinked at her then shook my head. "I don't understand."

"I mean, it's not just that you have to make this choice now, under duress like you said, but that you have to make this choice – and the shadow is how you're being forced to make it."

I squinted, trying to see what she meant. "Do you mean the reason I'm having all these weirdo problems is because I need to make this choice between being a 'witch', or whatever it is, and being just normal? And I need to decide now?"

Milly grinned at me. "That's exactly it."

I let it sink in; it did make sense. Perfect sense. It was also stupid and annoying – someone, somewhere was forcing my hand, if this was true. Was someone making all these horrible things happen to force me to choose some crazy path that had nothing to do with me?

I could feel my skin getting hotter and hotter as I stood up and went to the window. The clouds to the east were reaching across the sky like fingers now, layers of charcoal and grey, tinted with gold where they met the last rays of the sun. I watched them creep their way across the sky, trying to get the anger that was boiling in my guts under control.

"Anne?" Milly said from behind me, but I didn't turn around.

I had been happy; I had known where I was going. Okay, I had been lonely, and there were things about my life, about myself, that I understood so much better now than I had only a month ago. But that wasn't the point, I told myself, grinding my teeth. The point was that this was being done to me; it was ruining my life just because of some ancient journal and all the stuff my ancestors did, which had nothing to do with me. It was so unfair.

"Anne?" Milly said again, and I heard her get to her feet and come to stand next to me. She laid the journal on the windowsill and looked out at the clouds in silence, then turned to me, her face a little pale. "You're kind of scaring me," she said, reaching out a hand and laying it on my arm. "Are you okay?"

I swallowed, forcing back tears, and nodded. "I'm fine," I said, coming to a decision.

"Good..."

"I need you to do something for me," I interrupted her, turning back to the room.

She nodded, following me. "What?"

I sat down on the bed and looked up at her. "I need you to watch over my body."

Her eyes widened. "No way – you can't do that," she said. "You don't know how!"

"I need to talk to Grandma," I told her, feeling all my anger, frustration and fear bursting to get out. "I'm going to the forest and I'm going to find her."

Milly stared at me with her mouth wide open, the journal sitting forgotten on the windowsill behind her. "But how?"

I wasn't sure myself, but I knew I could do it. I knew it in my bones. All I had to do was try.

"Just stay here and watch over me." I caught her eye. "Will you do that?"

She hesitated, her mouth open to speak again. But the look on my face stopped her. She nodded.

"Thank you."

I lay back on the bed and closed my eyes, slowing my breathing as my pulse raced in my throat.

"Here," I heard Milly say, and I felt her lay something heavy under my hand. I closed my fingers around the worn leather binding of the journal and let the darkness come for me.

TWENTY-FOUR

I opened my eyes and fell out of the reeling darkness. Firm, smooth snow broke the fall. It was still daytime, bright and cold, and tiny flakes were drifting down between the trees. I steadied myself, got to my feet and began to walk, not thinking about the direction, just knowing I had to go forward.

The forest was silent and empty; nothing stirred. I could feel no shadow or presence around me and the snow beneath my bare feet was like silk, cool and soft instead of raw and biting. I was too angry to enjoy the beauty of it; in the back on my mind, I knew I didn't have long. My body was lying on my bed at home and soon Mum would come home and expect me up. I pressed onward, forcing myself to focus on what I wanted to achieve here.

I called out for my Grandmother and my voice echoed through the trees. I knew what Tierne had told me about the dead visiting the living, but it didn't matter; I needed to speak to her right now. She had to come.

I walked on, panting as I hurried. My breath was thick in the freezing air as it made the snowflakes sparkle and dance. I didn't know how much time had passed in the real world, and

I knew that Grandmother's fire was a long way off. But no matter how quickly I walked, it seemed like nothing changed. Tree after tree, the forest simply moved around me.

I stopped, rubbing my hands together. I tried to work out what I was doing wrong, but I couldn't think properly. Between the tree tops above me, the sky was darkening; clouds swirled like ink, throwing shadows across the snow at my feet. I stared up at them, my mind blank.

I had to keep moving, but there was no strength left in my legs; I realised that my toes were turning numb, my fingers too. I brushed hair out of my face and a gust of wind sent snow swirling around me, biting into the back of my neck. Something was wrong. I shuddered as sickness flowed through me, making my head spin.

I wondered what was happening to my body and hoped Milly was okay. It had been a stupid idea to come here like this, full of anger, not knowing what I was doing. Shaking my head, I tried to dislodge the doubts and took another slippery step forward.

The air was darkening quickly now; there was no colour of dusk to it though, no gold or rose tinge to the clouds, just grey heaviness above me. The forest seemed to close in as the shadows grew around me until I could barely see even the closest trees.

I was breathing fast now, gripping tree trunks as I passed them to stop myself from falling. It was too late, I thought, not knowing why I thought it. But it was true; it was too late. I'd left it too late and now there was no help to be had.

I still couldn't feel any presence nearby, but my heart thumped like it was going to burst anyway. My mouth was dry and my lips cracked painfully as I called into the heavy silence.

"Tierne!"

My voice was deadened by the snow, hardly making any noise. I didn't have any breath to call again, but kept on walking instead. The snowflakes fell heavier, swirling around me and obscuring the ground ahead. I rubbed my arms against my body, trying to warm myself up.

"You shouldn't have come like this," a low voice rumbled, making me jump and stumble sideways. I grabbed hold of the nearest tree and peered through the darkness. Only a few feet from me, a great bear face was staring at me. His eyes were dark, fearsome coals.

I gasped, unable to speak. Tierne watched me, sniffing the air as he waited for me to catch my breath. I swallowed a mouthful of cold air, felt it burn my lungs, then spoke.

"I was angry," I said, feeling stupid. "I wanted to talk to Grandma..."

My voice trailed away; it sounded so small in the forest. I swallowed again and wrapped my arms around my shaking shoulders. I took a step towards him.

"What should I do?"

He was sniffing the air, swinging his great head from left to right as though smelling something on the wind. For a few moments, he didn't reply. I stood watching him, trying to stop shivering.

"Follow me," he said at last, turning into the darkness and slipping away in total silence. I glanced around then followed him.

We walked through what felt like unending shadows. Time passed so slowly that I had to fight to stay awake as I hurried after the silent shape ahead of me. Tierne led me deeper and deeper into the forest – further than I'd ever been before – until at last the trees parted and we reached a frozen river, it's banks inky in the almost total darkness.

Tierne stopped and turned to look at me. Against the sky, I could see just how huge he was, and it made me hesitate. But I came and stood beside him, looking down at the dark sweep of frozen water.

"This is where you return," he said. Then he turned and faced the forest behind us.

I looked up at him, feeling frustrated, stupid, and grateful. I reached out a hand to touch him, then thought better of it.

"What do I do?" I whispered, and he turned his huge head to look down at me. I wondered if he was smiling or snarling at me.

"Cross the river," he said, "and you will be home."

I glanced at the icy waters and shuddered. "And then?"

He snorted, beginning to pad away on his giant paws. "Then, it's your choice..." he said over his shoulder as he vanished into the trees. A moment passed. "You'll have to make it fast after this," he added from the darkness.

I stared at the place he had disappeared, my heart sinking. I wanted to call for him again, to ask if he'd still help me, but I knew he was gone. So I turned back to the river and with a deep breath, I slipped a foot down onto the ice, wincing as it creaked beneath my weight. Then I stepped out towards home.

TWENTY-FIVE

It was stranger than anything I'd seen yet. Instead of darkness welling up around me as though I'd fallen asleep, light bloomed, growing until it almost blinded me. I kept moving forward, not knowing if I even had feet anymore, focusing on home as hard as I could.

And then I was gasping as a rush of warmth flooded my body. I sat up, heaving in great lungfuls of air as I blinked against the bright light. There was no one there.

I slid to the edge of the bed, my heart thumping hard. Where was Milly? A glance at the clock told me that only five minutes had passed since I'd lain down; it was still too early for Mum to be home yet and Milly had hours before she had to be home. I took a deep breath. There would be a normal reason for this, I tried to tell myself. Milly had probably gone to get something from downstairs when she saw I was stirring. I clung to this idea and pushed myself to my feet, about to go and look for her.

Then I heard a sound from the hallway and froze where I stood. It had just been one sob, but it gave me shivers all through my bones just hearing it. I stepped as quietly as I could towards the door and pulled it open, just wide enough to see out. The hallway beyond was in darkness. I stood there with shaking legs, willing myself to go on, when I heard it again.

I pulled the door a little wider and took a step out onto the landing. After the brightness of my room, it took my eyes a few minutes to adjust to the shadows. Another step forward and I could see around the chest beside my mum's bedroom door. Huddled on the floor in the corner, I could just make out a small shape. All my caution vanished and I ran to kneel beside it.

"Milly," I said, reaching out with both hands to take hold of her shoulders. She was bundled into the corner, as small as it was possible to curl, with her face pressed into the floor and her hands around her head. Tears came to my eyes as I struggled to lift her up to face me.

"Milly," I said again, but she just sobbed and tried to hide her face. I looked at her for a moment, forcing myself to be calm; I had to think.

"Milly, I'm going to turn the light on," I said, getting my feet underneath me so I could stand up. But she reached out and clung to my leg, almost pulling me over. Flinging my arms wide, I managed to reach the light switch. Nothing happened. I tried it again, but no lights came on. My stomach lurched, but I took a deep breath and forced myself to crouch down to her again.

"Okay," I said, sounding far more confident than I felt, "we're going back to my room. Come on."

I reached under her shoulders and stood up, pulling her upright with me. She buried her face into my arm and stumbled after me as I lead her through the darkness back to my bedroom, my heart hammering in my chest.

I slammed the door shut behind us. It shut out the darkness of the corridor and, with that, I realised how cold the house was. After the snowy forest, it had seemed like a furnace in here when I'd woken up, but now – now I could understand why Milly was shivering.

"Here," I said, pulling a blanket from the bed and wrapping her up in it. She stared at me, her face pure white, and I pushed her backwards to sit on the bed. Then I began to think. What had Tierne said – I wouldn't have much time to make my choice, after my trip to the forest. What had he meant?

I backed away from the bed, my mind spinning. There was a puzzle in front of me and I only had to fit one more piece, but how? What was I missing? Frustration boiled inside me and I clenched my fists; if only I'd been able to talk to Grandma, I thought, but it was no use. Getting angry had done me no good before, and it would only make this worse.

I took a deep breath and looked down at Milly. She was still shaking, but her face had more colour in it and she was watching me closely. "Are you okay?" I asked, crouching in front of her to look up into her face. She swallowed then nodded. "What happened?"

She didn't answer at first and I forced myself to be patient. This was my fault, whatever it was – that much was clear. There was no point getting frustrated with Milly too.

"I don't know," she said at last. "You went to sleep, that's all. But it wasn't right, something was wrong. You were cold. Really, really cold..."

She looked into my eyes and I felt my heart wrench with guilt at how tired and scared she looked.

"I sat and watched you, and for a minute nothing happened. Then..." she took a deep breath before going on, "then the lights went out. It was pitch dark. And I knew, I just knew, it was here – that thing."

I nodded, taking her hand and waiting for her to go on.

"I couldn't see it, but the room was cold, freezing. You were just lying there, and I couldn't stop thinking that you were dead. It seemed so real – it didn't even occur to me to think otherwise."

I could feel the temperature dropping around us. Milly glanced around the room.

"I could hear it laughing," she said. I had to lean close to hear her. "It said things – said it was my fault. Then it, it...." She shuddered, gripping my hand and letting her tears spill onto her lap.

"It what?" I said, feeling terrible for forcing her to go on, but knowing we didn't have much time left.

"It touched me," she said, and the look on her face was one of total disgust. I stared at her and she nodded. "It touched me."

I shook my head. This was new; it had never done anything like this before. I blew out a breath and it misted the air between us. Milly moaned at the sight of it, and I pushed my own fear deep down within me.

This was what Tierne had meant. Somehow, I had opened the door wider; maybe with my anger, maybe by going to the forest without knowing what I was doing. However I had done it, I had sealed my own fate. There was nothing else for me to do now, and I knew it.

I felt a grim satisfaction. Going to the forest had been my own choice, not anyone else's – that was something. I got to my feet, letting Milly's hand fall. The room was bitterly cold now; it bit into my face almost badly as the forest snow, but I didn't care.

"What are you going to do?" Milly whispered, watching me with wide eyes.

"Where's Grandma's journal?" I asked, scanning the room.

She hesitated, then drew the book out from under her jumper and offered it up to me. "Thanks."

I took the book and sat with it at the desk. I knew it would show me what I needed to know now that I was ready. It lay, innocent in my hands, and I whispered my question to it. "Show me how to make this choice."

Then I held it by the spine, allowed it to fall open, and began to read.

TWENTY-SIX

"A ceremony requires three simple elements," Grandma's handwriting read. "A form of containment, such as a circle drawn in the air with smoke. A representation of the Spirit, in whatever form feels appropriate. And a symbolic action to represent the intent of the ceremony."

I read hurriedly, knowing time was short. My fingers were growing numb on the edges of the page and I forced myself to ignore the icy feeling creeping into my stomach. A ceremony, the book was telling me. I had asked how to make the choice and it had taken me to a page about how to do a ceremony. That's pretty clear, I thought. But how on earth could I do a ceremony on such short notice?

I rubbed my hands together to warm them and glanced over my shoulder to check on Milly. She had edged backwards until she was leaning against the wall, but her eyes were open. She was very still, watching me. "You're going to do it, aren't you?"

I caught her eye and nodded. She grinned at me in spite of her fear. "How?"

I turned on the chair, holding the book open in my lap. "I don't know – the book's telling me about ceremonies," I said, waving at the open page. She gestured for me to bring it over to her and I sat beside her. It didn't take her long; she looked at me, sitting up a little straighter.

"This is pretty clear," she said. Thank God she was here with me, I thought.

"You need something to mark the circle. Anything will do."

"What about ribbon?" I asked, reaching over to pull some out of my bedside drawer.

"Fine."

I stuffed it into a pocket and she traced the next line with a finger.

"And you need a candle; I reckon that'll be the best representation of Spirit. What do you think?"

It made sense, I thought; I barely knew what Spirit was right now, but light and warmth sounded just right. I had a lighter in my desk drawer, and I dug it out as she went on.

"And you need to do something – to change something," she said, wrinkling her brow and looking at me. I stood up and waited for her to suggest something, but she shook her head. "No, I think you have to decide on that bit," she said.

"Yeah, I think so too."

I put the lighter in my pocket with the ribbon, then slipped the book from her hands and read the next bit of instructions.

"First, the space is created by making the boundary. Then the Spirit or spirits are called by name and asked for their help and guidance. Then, the action is performed."

That was pretty clear too, I thought with relief.

"Once the action is done, thank the Spirit for its help and break the boundary of the circle."

It seemed simple enough, I thought, my stomach churning.

I wondered if I was missing something; there had to be more to it than that.

Milly took the book from me and read that last part while I thought. What was I going to do to represent my intent? It needed to be something meaningful – I knew that much. And I didn't have much time to think about it either; the clock told me Mum would be home within the hour, and that wasn't the worst of my problems. The room was so cold now that the window was growing ferns of ice across the glass. The bed covers beneath Milly cracked as she breathed, as though the moisture in them was freezing. Even more worrying, the light above us was dimming, I was sure of it; the writing in the book was becoming harder to read as a gloom settled around us.

I glanced at Milly, hoping she hadn't noticed. She looked up at me in silence, closing the book with an air of finality.

This was it then. I got to my feet, looking around, but it just didn't feel right to stay in that room. I glanced at the doorway, shuddering at the thought of the darkness beyond it, and Milly took my hand.

"You're right," she said, looking around us at the gathering shadows. "We can't stay here."

I tried to smile at her and felt my cheeks ache with cold. "Come on."

I lead her to the door, holding her hand in mine while she used the other one to clutch the journal and her blanket to her chest.

"Don't suppose you've got a torch?" she said with a dry laugh.

I shook my head. "No, and I don't think it would do any good anyway."

She nodded and took a deep breath.

I closed my eyes for just a moment, hoping Tierne and

Grandma were helping us, then pulled the door open. Freezing air rushed in at us, taking my breath away, and I stepped forward, dragging Milly behind me.

Out of the corner of my eye, I could see deep drifts of snow around our feet that disappeared when I looked straight at them. My toes felt it too; they throbbed with cold as we hurried to the top of the stairs.

"Keep moving," I whispered to Milly over my shoulder, and she squeezed my hand.

Going down the steps, we had to be careful not to slip on the ice that wasn't there. It was like a dream, a twilight world of snow and ice overlaid on top of my normal home. I couldn't let myself think about it; there was a pressure in my mind like weight against a locked door. It was all I could do to keep us moving.

Reaching the ground floor, I sucked in a deep breath and looked around. It was warmer down here and my fingers ached as they started to defrost. I hadn't realised how chilled and stiff they'd gotten as we sat in my bedroom.

We made our way through the darkness of the living room, ignoring the whispers at the back of my mind. It didn't matter what doubts I had now; I had made my decision. It was the only thing I could do, I told myself. But another part of me didn't agree; a voice in my mind argued I was throwing my life away, messing with things I didn't understand. Did I even know Grandma and Tierne were real? Maybe I was ill, hallucinating, or it was a trick – had I thought about that?

My steps slowed. I came to a stop in the middle of the room and Milly came up beside me, her pale face eerie in the shadows.

"What's wrong?" she asked, and I barely heard her words against the voice in my head. Maybe she was in on it, it suggested. I stared at her, unable to think.

"Hey!" She pulled on my hand, jerking me sideways. I staggered towards her then caught my balance. This wasn't me, I told myself. They weren't my thoughts at all. Anger filled me. I reached out into the darkness, not knowing what I was doing, and felt a wave of strength run through me, dispelling the cold inertia.

"Go away!" I yelled, turning around and glaring into the shadows. "Leave me alone!"

There was a whirl of air against our faces as though we'd opened a window in a gale, and then the living room light flashed back to full brightness.

I felt like I'd been struck. Grabbing Milly with both hands and ignoring the stricken look on her face, I pulled her towards the back door. We passed a book shelf on the way, and my heart leapt; a tea light in a glass holder was tucked between the books – one of Mum's favourites. I grabbed it and shoved it into my pocket without stopping. Then, wrenching the door open, I stumbled out into the evening air.

It was warm; the sky was a pale grey and the bushes were rippling in a soft breeze. I turned and pulled Milly through the doorway, then slammed it shut behind her. We stood, panting on the grass as the shakes left us.

Milly caught my eye. "What the hell was that?" she asked, half-laughing and half-sobbing. I breathed slowly through my nose, trying not to burst out laughing as well. I was feeling reckless, wild; I had sent it away – I had power against it.

I span and collapsed on the grass a few feet away, waving for her to join me.

"That was scary," I said, leaning back on my trembling arms to look up at the sky.

She dropped the blanket to the ground, then stood over me.

"What happened?"

"I don't know. I just – it was talking to me again. I couldn't think. But I felt different." I laughed and sat up. "I told it to go away!"

Milly sat down, setting the journal on the ground in front of us. She blew out a long breath and pushed her hair back over her shoulder. "This is crazy," she said, and I laughed again; great, heaving breaths of laughter that felt more like sobs.

It was hard to get a hold of myself. Relief was pouring out of me; it felt so good to be out of the cold. Maybe that's all I needed to do, I thought for a moment. Then I dismissed the idea. I knew without thinking that as soon as I went back in the house I would have exactly the same problem again – I had run out of time. If I didn't start getting some help from Tierne, I would be in big trouble. And so would Milly and my mum.

That thought sobered me up quicker than anything else. Mum would be home soon. I couldn't let her walk into a half-world of ice and snow; I had no idea what effect it might have on her. I glanced at Milly beside me and she was sitting with her chin in her palm, watching me with a deep frown. All signs of her fear from earlier was gone, and once again I was struck by how strong she was. I only hoped I could be that strong.

I shifted on the grass, brushing my fingers across the binding of the journal and feeling a hard resolve come into me. I stood up and dug my hands into my pockets, drawing out the lighter, the candle and the ribbon. And with these ordinary items came something else, something that glittered in my palm in the fading light, making me smile.

"What is it?" Milly asked, leaning forward to see.

I lowered my hand to reveal the old, green ring Grandma had made. I had forgotten it was in my pocket – or maybe it hadn't been in there at all. But it was here now, and I felt like this was where I had always needed to be. I wasn't alone.

I caught Milly's eye and we both nodded. There was no need to talk. I stepped around her in a slow circle, laying the ribbon on the grass and knowing as I did so that the ceremony had begun. The evening slowed and hushed; the sounds of traffic faded to nothing as though we were standing in a forest glade rather than my garden. I looked up and saw the first stars of the evening blinking down at me and knew I was being watched.

I sat down. In the centre of the circle, Milly set the candle on the grass. It gleamed a little as the last of the daylight met the glass. I closed my eyes, clasping the lighter in my hand, and felt it coming to me: a wave of knowing that had always been there right on the edge of my life. It came up through me like water through tree roots, flooded over me like light from the sun; warmed every part of me. And in the stillness that came with it, I knew without any doubt that I was in the presence of Spirit.

I opened my eyes and bent forward to light the candle. It flared then settled to a low flicker that danced in the breeze. I watched it for a moment with unexpected gratitude in my heart. I had never felt safe and peaceful in my whole life. I was home.

I looked up into Milly's face. The candle light threw a golden glow across her features, making her beautiful. With her long hair loose around her shoulders and the darkening sky above her, she looked more like a witch than anything I'd ever seen. I smiled and her eyes sparkled.

I stood up again. With my face to the sky, I took a deep, slow breath. This was the moment. After this, there was no turning back. I knew what I was about to do, that it would change my life forever, and I was surprised to find I was okay with that now. Deep inside me, I had always known it would come to this, and whether the shadow was here to force me into it or not didn't matter anymore. Because nothing was changing; this was me – who I was deep down in my soul –and all I did tonight was accept that fact.

Lying in my open palm, Grandma's ring shone with candlelight. I held it up and realised that it had changed; the etchings on the inside were stronger now, clearly showing the outline of a great bear. I smiled, greeting Tierne and welcoming him to the circle. The green stone was translucent now and deep within it I could see movement, faces. Grandma was watching me as well.

Without thinking about it, I held up the ring to the evening sky, offering it to the trees, the stars, the earth, the candle light and the clouds that were fading in the East, and then with them all as witnesses, I slipped it onto my middle finger. It fit as though it were made for me.

For a single moment, I could feel the whole world beneath my skin and I knew that my decision was rippling out from me, changing everything. Then time resumed and I looked down at Milly, who was grinning and crying as she shielded the candle from the breeze. I grinned too.

It was over; I bent down and blew out the candle, feeling a little reluctant to lose that wonderful feeling of peace. Then I reached out for Milly's hand and she rose to stand beside me. There was a pause, and then we lifted the ribbon from the grass, breaking the circle and ending the ceremony.

The sounds of the town came back as though someone had turned up the radio. We looked around and I tried to take it all in. Then I heard the front door slam, and my heart jumped up my throat.

The stillness vanished as Milly and I looked at each other in horror, the spell of silence broken. We rushed to the back door and into the house. There was no coldness, no ice or snow in the corners of our eyes; just Mum taking off her shoes and smiling as we hurried into the hallway.

"Hi, girls," she said, shrugging off her coat and hanging it up. "How was your day?"

I put out a hand to hold onto the railing of the stairs as my strength left me. Suddenly, I felt like I'd run a marathon three times over.

I watched Mum's face change as she saw me. "What have you been doing?" she asked, gripping my arm to stop me falling as she put a hand on my forehead. I shook my head, but I could barely think, let alone speak. Mum turned to Milly, her face stern. "What's been going on here?" she asked while Milly stared at me in clear confusion.

She shook her head. "I don't know," she said, peering at me. "She was fine a minute ago. We were just in the garden, that's all..."

I nodded, trying to back her up as I let them both take me by the arms.

Mum looked at me. "And what has she been doing all day?"

"I don't know, I only got here an hour ago," Milly explained. "Mum went out."

Mum raised her eyebrows, but the lecture about sneaking out behind my aunt's back could apparently wait. She led me into the kitchen and forced me into a chair. "Has she eaten?"

Milly shrugged, shaking her head. "I think she just over did it, just then when she rushed in to meet you," she said, trying to sound as convincing as possible. "She'd been sitting down the whole time before that."

She caught my eye. Mum glared at us as she poured a cup of tea and set it in front of me. I could tell she didn't believe us, but she seemed to be more interested in making me feel better than interrogating me.

"Drink that," she said, putting a hand on my shoulder and peering into my face. I realised I must look terrible for her to be so worried. I put my hands around the hot cup and took a sip.

The hot, sweet tea helped, and so did sitting down. After a few minutes I was feeling well enough to creep up the stairs and crawl into bed. Mum seemed to have given up asking Milly for an explanation and she focused on cooking us some dinner instead while I lay down with strict instructions to do nothing at all. I didn't mind the fuss, to be honest; I felt so used up that I wasn't interested in anything other than lying down and thinking over everything that had happened.

My skin was cool and sticky as though I had a fever, and although my head wasn't aching it did feel strange –like it might just float off my neck. Milly slid Grandma's journal into my desk without Mum seeing, then perched herself on my chair to watch me. She brought the blanket up from the garden, pretending it had been for me all along, and now it was lying across my legs, warming me up.

After a while she leaned forward, glancing at the door, and whispered, "Are you all right?"

I caught her eye and nodded once. Just that small movement made the room spin.

"Did it work?" she asked, and again I nodded. I was certain of that. I could feel something new growing inside me.

"I'd better go home," she said after a while. "Will you be okay?"

I smiled at her. "Yeah," I croaked. "Thanks."

She shrugged, but her grin said it all.

I listened as she made her way downstairs and explained to Mum that she'd better leave. My aunt would be back by now; Milly was already going to be in trouble. I heard Mum sigh then they closed the kitchen door and I couldn't hear any more. The next thing I knew, Mum was pushing open my bedroom door with a tray of steaming food.

"Here," she said, putting down the tray on the end of the bed and handing me the drink. "How are you feeling?"

I shrugged. I wasn't going to go into just how drained I felt; it would only worry her more. She stared at me as I took a sip and put down the glass, then handed me a bowl full of soup. I tucked in, ignoring the look she was giving me and concentrating instead on how the food was warming me up from the inside out.

"I still don't understand what made you so tired," she said, shaking her head and sitting down in the chair. I swallowed another mouthful and looked at her. It was so tempting to tell her the truth, but I still wasn't sure how she'd take it. I caught her eye and saw that she knew I was holding back. The disappointment on her face made me feel ill all over again.

"I'm sorry." I put down the spoon. "I don't mean to worry you."

She gave me a hard look. "I do believe that," she said. "But I am worried. You said you'd tell me what was going on."

I swallowed, trying to get rid of the lump in my throat. After everything that had happened today, I didn't think I could cope with this too.

"I'm sorry," she said, seeing my eyes well with tears as I tried to think of something to say.

I shook my head. "No, Mum. Don't be sorry – I'm sorry." I leaned back to rest my head on the pillow. It was taking so much energy just to sit up and talk.

"You will tell me though, won't you? When you're ready."

I tried to nod, but all I could manage was a grimace.

Mum shook her head at me and took the bowl from my

hands, putting her palm against my forehead. "You're too hot," she said. "I think you've got a fever."

The room was spinning as though I'd just stepped off a fair ride. Mum's eyes narrowed. "Right, that's it," she said, spinning on her heal and heading for the door. "I'm going to call work and tell them I can't come in tomorrow – there's no way you're going to school."

I tried to tell her I'd be fine with some sleep, but the words wouldn't come out. I didn't even feel hungry anymore; my body felt like it was sinking into a bath of feathers. I let myself slip down the pillow until I was slumped, half-lying on the pillows, and with the smell of soup and bread and my mother filling my mind, I closed my eyes.

TWENTY-SEVEN

I was half expecting to find myself in the forest again. Even in my exhaustion, I knew that Tierne and Grandma would want to talk to me. So I was surprised when I realised that, instead of snow and bare trees, I was surrounded by stone. The ground beneath my feet was uneven, cool and gritty, and as I moved it scuffed beneath my feet.

Putting out my hand, I felt the cool stone walls arching above my head to form a cave. I could hear the soft breathing of the bear, Tierne, and the murmur of voices. I smiled. "Hello again."

The light resolved out of the darkness into a small fire encircled by stones on the cave floor. Grandma was sitting beside it, framed by the dark mouth of the cave. Her smile was broad, warm as the firelight that danced across her features as she sat cross-legged on the bare stone.

I glanced at the huge shape to my left. Tierne was beyond the reach of the fire's glow, with only his eyes distinct in the shadows as he watched me. I swallowed, feeling awkward, and nodded to him. How should you greet a bear?

Grandma laughed at me and the sound bounced off the

walls around us for a moment

"You did well," she said. I turned from Tierne to face her. There were other murmurings around us, rippling and dancing with the crackling of the fire. I peered into the shadows for a moment, trying to see who else was there.

"This is the meeting place," Grandma went on, calling back my attention. "When you come here, you can speak with any of us – spirit or ancestor."

I frowned, peering over her shoulder again to try and get a glimpse of who was whispering back there. Then I shook my head. "I don't understand – what do you mean by spirit or ancestor? Aren't they the same thing?"

In the shadows, the great bear stirred and there was soft humph. Grandma chuckled.

"No and yes."

But I didn't feel as intimidated as I had before; I had figured it out, hadn't I? I had done the ceremony, gotten rid of the shadow. I deserved some answers. Grandma grinned as though she knew exactly what I was thinking. She waved her hand for me to go on and sat waiting until I was ready.

"How can the answer be no and yes?" I asked. "Do you mean an ancestor is a spirit, but that a spirit isn't necessarily an ancestor?"

I knew as I said it that it was the right answer. Grandma chuckled again, and I sat up a little straighter, pleased with myself.

"I did the ceremony," I said, deciding to get on with why I was there. Grandma nodded. "I'm part of this now?" I went on.

"You are part of our lineage, yes."

"But what does that mean, really?"

To my left, there was a scraping and rustling, and then the

stone beneath me shook as Tierne heaved himself to his paws. He came to stand in the circle of firelight, his huge, dark eyes glinting at me.

"It means," he said, making dust fall from the cave ceiling, "that you have accepted who you are."

I stared at him, waiting for him to go on. Instead, he lowered himself down beside Grandma, making her seem tiny, and put his head back down onto his paws. I swallowed my nerves, hesitated, and then turned back to Grandma, feeling a little nervous of making him say anything else.

"Um, okay..." I said, trying to phrase what I wanted to ask.

Grandma laughed out loud, interrupting me. "It means nothing, only what you choose for it to mean." She caught my eye and held it steadily. In the light and shadows of the fire, I felt a sudden sense of awe at the thought I was talking so someone who'd done all this and more long before me. In some ways, she was more daunting than Tierne.

I dragged my thoughts back to what she'd just said, more confused than ever.

"Do you mean it was only for me – for my own benefit? That I needed to do it so I knew what I wanted, what I decided?" I asked.

Tierne huffed again, making sparks fly from the embers of the fire.

"That's all? It doesn't bind me to anything, or change me?"

I couldn't believe it; I had felt so sure I was doing something important and now all that struggle seemed pointless. But Grandma shook her head.

"Don't think it wasn't important," she said. "It was. It was the most important thing you've ever done." Her eyes flashed as she went on. "This was the first decision you've ever truly made for yourself. You accepted where you were, who you are, what you feel, and where your path has led you so far – you accepted your heritage and what you are deep in your soul. Does there need to be something more important than that?"

I stared at her. She was right; it was a huge deal. I had just expected it to, I don't know, give me special powers or something.

Grandma laughed and shook her head, and once again I wondered if she could hear my thoughts. "By accepting your nature and where it has led you, you did claim a special power," she said, leaning forward and looking straight into my face. My heart beat against my ribs; if all that changed was my knowledge of myself – my acceptance of myself – I wondered, how could that give me any kind of power?

"You claimed your power. The power of being you, of being who you are," she said. In the shadows, her eyes sparkled like stars.

"But what is that?" I whispered.

Grandma shrugged. "We'll see," she said, sitting back again and smiling at Tierne.

I didn't dare ask her again. The fire was leaping higher and higher. I could make out the first stirrings of dawn across the forest behind her as the sky became not black, but the darkest of greys. I had to find out as much as I could while I had time.

"What do I do now?" I asked, looking from one of them to the other.

Grandma sat back, her face disappearing into flickering shadow as she turned to Tierne. I winced as his great bulk stirred again, shaking the rock walls and making the flames jump and spiral. He raised his head until it was level with mine and stared at me through the flames.

"You must win your freedom from the shadow," he said. I could feel his eyes on me as he said it, and I felt a flush of exasperation go through me; why couldn't they just explain properly? The corners of his muzzle twitched, flashing sharp white teeth, and I wondered if he was smiling.

"But it's gone," I said, amazed that I was brave enough to contradict him.

He shook his great head at me. "It only withdrew out of your world when you took the choice," he said as though explaining something simple to a toddler. "It hunts you still, through the forest. You will not be safe traveling in this world until you are free of it."

I stared at him, not understanding what he meant. "So it didn't really leave when I did the ceremony?" I asked.

"It left your world because you became more powerful than it there, once again," he said. "It knows it can't harm you there now."

I felt a flood of relief. "Do you mean it can't come back to my house again?"

Tierne nodded. I sighed; one less thing to worry about.

"It will stalk you in the night instead," he went on, breaking me out of my bubble of relief. "In your dreams, and in the half-state between sleep and waking."

My stomach churned at this thought; I had assumed it had just gone when I did the ceremony. That something magical had happened just from me choosing this path.

I looked up into Tierne's face, more confused and daunted than ever. "But, why is it chasing me?" I asked, trying to sound braver than I felt.

He chuckled, making the floor shake beneath me, and a ripple ran through the shadows behind him as though the forest itself was listening. "You know why," he said.

"I don't! Milly thought maybe it was to make me make the choice, to force me into this situation, or I thought maybe it was so I didn't make this choice – that seems to be what the shadow itself wanted." I looked up at him, feeling utterly drained. "I'm so confused."

Tierne laughed again, making my ears ring. Then he shook his head and sat up on his hind legs so he towered above me. "You're doing well," he said, and I was surprised at how soft and kind his voice could be.

I blinked back tears and nodded, even though I didn't agree. "But what do I do now?" I asked again.

"Go home," he said, "and I will come to help you when the shadow returns – don't be scared, just call for me and I'll find you. I'll help you."

I nodded. I was exhausted and overwhelmed. Somehow, I had assumed that making my choice would be the end of all this fear, of being hunted. Finding out that it wasn't over was so disappointing and I wasn't even sure what I needed to do next. The fire began to swim in front of me, and I knew I was going home again. I wondered if I should ask anything else, but I was just too tired; I needed to rest, to figure out what had happened, and to talk it all through with Milly. Then a thought occurred to me.

I peered through the gloom and met Tierne's unreadable eyes. "Can I tell my Mum about all this?"

I had to shout over the roaring in my ears. There was a moment when thought I was already too far away to hear his answer, and then it rolled over me like a tidal wave, sweeping me back to my body with just one word: "Yes."

TWENTY-EIGHT

The rest of that night was a dark and comfortable blank. I woke on Monday morning to find the sun already high in the sky and the house quiet. I lay beneath the covers, so relaxed that my limbs felt detached from me, and remembered my dream.

It wasn't strange anymore, how clear and real these dreams were. Over the last few weeks, the world of the forest had become as real and normal as the normal world. Looking back, I could feel all of the pieces – all of my experiences of the last few days, the last few weeks – coming together. It was beginning to make sense to me.

I smiled and stretched, enjoying the soft coolness of the sheets. Downstairs, Mum was speaking on the phone, and I could just make out her voice coming through the kitchen door. I sighed; even though Tierne had told me I could tell her, and even with how much I longed to have her support, it was a nerve wracking idea. How was I going to explain it and would she believe me? Or would she be even more worried and cart me off to the doctor again? But it was a risk I was going to have to take; I couldn't hide all of this from her anymore and

I didn't want to. I would just have to trust that Tierne knew better than me.

I sat up and smoothed my hair back out of my face. I was a mess; I couldn't remember the last time I'd had a shower or brushed my teeth, and I hadn't worn anything but pyjamas since Friday. It would make me feel more like myself to get into some proper clothes and run a brush through my hair.

I slipped out of bed and grabbed some clothes from the wardrobe, being as quiet as I could so Mum didn't hear me. I didn't want her to come up and insist I get back into bed. I didn't need to worry though. She was still talking on the phone and it wasn't until I'd had a shower, dressed and was almost downstairs that I heard her put it down.

I headed straight for the kitchen, pushing the door open and trying to hitch a normal expression onto my face. "Good morning," I said, glancing at the clock. It was coming up to 11'o'clock – I had slept for over 12 hours.

Mum looked up from the papers that were spread all over the table. She smiled at me, but there were dark circles under her eyes.

"How are you feeling?" she asked as she got to her feet.

I waved for her to sit down. "I'm fine." I pushed her back into her chair and went to get myself something to eat. She watched me in silence for a minute, and I tried to let my new feeling of energy show.

"I'm sorry you couldn't go to work," I said, sitting down opposite her.

She cleared a space on the table for my bowl, shrugging. "That's all right – you're more important than all this." She gestured at all the paperwork. I knew she meant it, but I hated seeing her like this.

"I really am okay," I told her. But she just frowned.

"Well, I've made an appointment with the doctor for this afternoon anyway," she said. "Just to make sure."

I held in a sigh. It was natural for her to worry – I knew that. I would just have to wait until later to tell her everything. I nodded and swallowed a mouthful of my breakfast. "Fine."

She gave me a sharp look. "You're okay with that?"

I shrugged.

"Yeah. I know there's nothing wrong with me, but I suppose it's sensible, isn't it? Just to make sure."

"Thanks, Love." She reached over and squeezed my fingers. I looked down at my food, knowing what was coming. This just wasn't the right time. She leaned forward, putting her hands palm down on the table between us. "So –"

"Has Milly called?" I said, interrupting her.

She eyed me for a moment, then shook her head. "No, I imagine she's at school though."

"Oh yeah."

I turned my gaze to the window, hoping she wouldn't try again. I couldn't think of anything else to distract her with. It was a beautiful day out there – one of the last sunny days of the year, judging by the crisp coolness in the air. I sighed, wishing I could get out into that sunshine as I stirred the food round my bowl.

Mum was frowning at me, but she didn't try to ask again. Through the relief, I felt a pang of guilt; she was trusting me to tell her the truth, and I kept putting her off. I just hoped that when I did finally tell her, it didn't disappoint her.

"I have to make some more calls," she said, taking my empty bowl. "Are you going to be okay on your own?"

"Mm Hmm." I yawned. If I was honest with myself, all I wanted to do right now was sit and think. It was a good thing I wasn't at school.

Mum ran a hand down my hair. "Great. Let me know if you need anything."

I got up to go then paused. "Mum?"

She turned from filling up the sink, already lost in thought. "Mmm?"

"I love you."

Her tired eyes crinkled as she smiled, but I didn't wait for her to say anything. I left the room and headed upstairs again, thanking the heavens she was so understanding.

The day passed in a blur. Before hardly any time had gone by, we were having lunch. Then Mum was hurrying me out of the door, bundled up in a coat and scarf against the wind, and into the car. I wasn't bothered when it came to it. After the last few days, it was just nice to be doing something normal where the only cold was from the turning weather and the only noises or shadows were completely mundane.

"I can't see anything the matter other than a bad virus," the doctor told us after prodding and poking me for twenty minutes. I had forced myself to be patient with him because of the look on Mum's face as she explained how I'd been feeling. I was glad she only knew about the tiredness and passing out, because just that much was enough to get me the third degree.

Finally satisfied, the doctor sat back in his chair to jab at his keyboard.

"There's nothing we can do for viruses," he went on. Mum nodded solemnly. "The best thing is lots of rest, good food and lots of water – and don't get cold."

I did my best not to smile at this last bit. If only he knew.

"And you're sure that's just it?" Mum asked.

"I'm sure. Obviously, if it goes on for more than a couple of weeks, we'll do some more tests." He peered at his screen. "But I can tell you now that all of Anne's results on Friday night were normal – all of them." He smiled again. "There's really nothing to worry about."

"Thank you," she said, getting to her feet. I leapt up to follow her, glad to be out of there.

"Feeling better already, aren't you?" he said, bobbing his head at me as he followed us to the door.

"Yeah." I left it at that.

Mum led me back to the car, fussing over my buttons to make sure the wind didn't get to my chest. When we were back in the sweltering car, she leaned over and patted my hand. "I know you hate the doctors," she said, starting up the engine, "so thanks for being patient."

I wondered if this was the time to tell her, but we were back on the road and Mum was concentrating on navigating through the traffic. Later, I told myself. Over a cup of tea. But I knew time was getting short – if I didn't tell her soon, something would happen and freak her out. That was the last thing we needed.

I didn't know how I knew, or even what I knew, but I could feel something building. Ever since after the ceremony last night, it was like the pressure had been off somehow; I'd had space to breathe. But now, not quite yet but soon, this period of calm would be over and I would have to act again. My stomach flipped at the thought and I forced myself to stop thinking about it. I just had to trust Tierne and Grandma, I told myself. They hadn't been wrong so far.

We drove the rest of the way in silence. Finally, the car swung around the corner and crept closer to our house. I caught Mum frowning in the mirror and I wondered if she was worrying about work. But there, parked in Mum's usual spot, was Dad's silver car, shining with polish.

Mum swore then glanced over at me. "Sorry," she said, blushing.

"I didn't hear a thing," I told her, but I couldn't help grinning. She grimaced back and her eyes looked sad rather than happy. She parked the car on the opposite side of our house then she turned to me. Over her shoulder, I could see Dad's car idling by the curb in front of our house.

"I had a feeling he might come to see you," she said. My confusion obviously showed on my face. "Your aunt said she might call him."

The penny dropped; he was here about Grandma's book. My whole body felt colder, tighter. I stared into Mum's face, feeling all the colour drain from my skin. "Mum," I whispered.

"It's okay; I'm going to back you up," she said, squeezing my arm. "Where's the book?"

I swallowed the enormous lump in my throat. "It's in my room, in my desk," I said, feeling stupid for leaving it somewhere so obvious. There was still so much I needed in there – I couldn't lose it. Tears stung my eyes and I blinked them away. "Do I have to talk to him?" I said, hoping she could use my 'illness' as an excuse to send him away.

She hesitated. "I'm sorry, but I think you do," she said, starting to gather up her coat and bag. "It'll be better to get it over with."

My legs felt like lead as I followed her out onto the street. The wind was howling like a raging voice; it tugged at my hair and whipped around my face. I took a slow breath and felt better for the clear, cold reality of it.

Mum strode across the road to Dad's waiting car and knocked on his window. He rolled it down, and I saw them say something to each other; the wind caught the words and threw them away in the space between us. I dragged my feet, wishing I was somewhere else and trying not to curse Aunt Sandy as I crossed the road to meet them.

Catching Mum's eye, I felt a fleeting steeliness pass between us. I may not have told her everything yet, but I knew right then that she was on my side.

Mum opened our front door and I followed her inside, ignoring my dad as he stamped and huffed on the doorstep, fighting with the wind. Finally, he managed to slam the door shut and turned to look at us.

"I'll put the kettle on," Mum said, and she walked into the kitchen, leaving me on my own with him. He shrugged off his coat and scooped me into a stiff hug. All I wanted was to walk away from him, There was nothing he could say about the book that I cared about, but Mum was right: that probably wouldn't help.

"Hi, Anne," he said into my hair. I let him hold me for a minute before I pulled away.

"Hi, Dad." I didn't look him in the eye. "We were at the doctors."

I wanted to play that card right away, hoping he'd think twice and leave. But it was only a small hope. Instead, he pointed to the kitchen, not even really hearing me.

"Shall we go and warm up?" he asked, heading off without me. I realised he wanted Mum there too; maybe this was more for her benefit than mine.

We all sat down around the kitchen table, behind the steaming mugs of tea Mum had poured. It was so ridiculous that I wanted to laugh. He was acting as though we didn't know why he was there.

He leaned back in his chair. "So, how've you been feeling?" he asked.

"Tired." I watched how his eyes slid around the room, not really looking at either of us. He had one hand in his pocket, and I could hear his keys clinking as he gripped them.

"I just thought I'd pop in to check on you, seeing as you had that fall on Friday night."

I shot a glance at Mum. She was scowling into her tea. At least Mum told me the truth, I thought. He's not even being honest with me, as usual. Looking at him across from me, it was like I was seeing him for the first time. His grey hair and skin and eyes made him looked only half-there, but he was grinning like a maniac at us, pretending not to notice the awkward silence that drifted between us like snow. I had never looked at him like this before, and I realised with a jolt he was just a man; there was no reason for us to make such a big deal out of what he said or thought.

I felt a shock of electricity go through me. In the last few days, I'd dealt with monsters and bears, I'd traveled to talk to the dead – was I going to let him intimidate me? I almost laughed again. Mum was staring at me, and with a wild feeling that was like wind whirling inside me, I winked at her.

She sat up a little straighter. I was surprised to see that Dad was still talking, and it was as though his voice was empty. Listening to the words, I realised why. He was talking about nothing, just going on about everything and anything other than what was actually on his mind.

"You can't have Grandma's journal," I said, looking him straight in the eye. Silence smashed around us and I smiled inside. I sat and waited for him to speak; this was a much better approach, I thought.

He stammered for a few moments and I wondered if he was going to ask what I was talking about. Then he got a grip on himself. "That's not your decision, I'm afraid," he said. His face had turned a paler shade of grey, but I just shook my head.

"It's certainly not yours," I said, and somewhere inside me I was stunned at how I was talking to him. I'd never spoken to an adult like this before in my whole life. His mouth fell open and his arms folded in front of his chest. The paleness of his face became a muddy pink, and he turned to Mum. "Jo," he began, but she held up a hand to stop him.

"Anne and I have discussed this," she said, "and I support her. She and Milly should know about their Grandma and their heritage."

Dad spluttered. "You have no idea what you're talking about." He was leaning so far forward that he was nearly out of his chair. "She was a dangerous woman, delusional –"

"You don't know that," I said. My hands were hot now, but my head felt cool and clear. "You didn't even listen to her!"

"You are far too young to know anything about this," he said, his face glowing. "She was crazy – our father thought so too. I don't know why he married her."

He was leaning over the table now. It reminded me of the bad times before he'd left. But I stared up into his reddening face and felt even calmer; it was like I was watching him from far away, and it had nothing to do with me. I even managed to feel a bit sorry for how upset this made him.

"I'm sorry, Dad," I said, keeping my voice soft. He nodded, folding his arms. "But it's my choice, and I've made it."

He stared at me in silence and I realised I'd said the one thing he could hear. His face drained of all colour then he gave me one tight little nod. "Fine. Fine," he said, standing up and taking a step away towards the door. "If that's how it's going to be…" He looked at Mum and sneered at her. "This is your fault," he said, almost spitting the words. "You can be freaks together then for all I care – I want nothing more to do with you."

His words clanged into place like an iron wall between us. I knew it was no use to try and talk with him anymore; he meant it and I knew there was no way I could change his mind. I stood up as well.

"I'm sorry about that," I said, feeling taller than I had ever felt before. "And if you ever change your mind, you know where we are."

He snorted, his nostrils flaring as he backed into the hallway. "Don't wait for a call." He grabbed his coat and slung in under his arm.

We followed him to the door. Neither of us said a thing as he banged it open, letting the wind roar into the house. With one last look over his shoulder, scowling as though he could burn his anger into us with just his eyes, he vanished into the dusk. A moment later we heard his car door slam.

Mum forced the door closed and I felt myself shrinking back into my normal self. I stepped forward hug her, feeling her arms shaking beneath mine.

"It's okay," I said. She nodded into my hair.

We stood like that for a long time, the house empty around us. And while we seemed to have lost someone from our lives for good, knowing that Mum believed in me made me feel less alone than ever.

TWENTY-NINE

It took a while to get calm again. My heart was pumping like I'd just fought for my life, and I must have looked like I felt because Mum sat me down in the kitchen and made a fresh pot of tea. When she sat down opposite me with the mugs, Mum was as pale and shaky as I was.

We looked at each other for a moment, and I knew that this was the moment.

"What did you mean when you said you'd made your choice?" Mum asked, beating me to it.

I examined the dregs of my tea.

"He knew what you meant, didn't he?"

"I think so, although I didn't mean it like that when I said it." I put down the cup and rubbed my eyes while I figured out what to say. "Or at least, I didn't think I did."

"I don't understand."

"I'm sorry," I said. "I should have talked to you about it days ago. I just..." I couldn't explain why I hadn't now; it seemed so long ago.

"It doesn't matter," she said so gently that my eyes started to sting. I reached over and took her hand in both of mine, looking her straight in the eye. This was it.

"Grandma was a witch," I said. "Or whatever it was called in her culture – she doesn't use the word 'witch' at all."

Mum stared at me, motionless; she looked like she was holding her breath.

"It's real, or at least there's something real that people like her knew about," I went on, measuring every word. "Her Grandmother was one too, and taught her. And there were others as well."

I couldn't tell what she was thinking, but I couldn't stop now. I had to tell her everything.

"She did believe Milly and I were like her – or could be." I hesitated.

"Go on," she whispered.

"She was right."

We looked at each other. Her eyes were wide and I could see, deep within them, a flash of the brilliant spark that I hadn't seen in so long.

I leaned forward to examine her face. "Are you all right?"

She gave a tight little nod. "Yes. Go on."

"What do you want to know?"

She pulled her hands from mine and threw them into the air. "How do you know all this?" Her face flushed. "What has been happening?"

I sat back and thought about how put it all into words. The bubble of quiet had burst; my stomach lurched as I wondered if this was about to go really wrong.

"She wrote about being able to travel into the forest, but without leaving this country," I told her. "She called it dreaming, and said she met with someone there, someone who taught her." I looked into her eyes, hoping Tierne was going to help me out. "I can do that. I have been doing that before I even knew what it was."

She let out a long breath, nodding and wiping tears from her eyes with the back of her hand.

I wondered if I should wait for her to speak, but she waved for me to go on.

"It started this summer," I began. It would be best to start at the beginning. She listened, hardly breathing as I described to her everything that had been happening, from the voice talking to me, to the coldness, the ring, the journal, the dreams of the forest, and finally what had happened in my dream last night.

But the time I had finished, the kitchen was dark. The words had been a flood, just pouring out of me without any thought at all; it felt good to be rid of them. I sat back in my chair and ran my hands over my face; a familiar aching pressure was building inside me again. Something was coming.

I looked up at her, wondering if she was ever going to speak to me again. She was nodding very slowly, looking at the table as though she was staring at something far away.

"I suppose," she said at last, "I've always hoped..." Then she went still, shutting her eyes tight. "I don't know what to say. I'm feeling a lot of things right now. I need to sort them out."

I hoped she wouldn't take too long. There was no coldness, no sense of the shadow near me, but there was something – something new and strange, pulling at me.

I sat in the darkness and waited for her to speak again. Watching her face, I could feel all the waves of emotion battling inside her. Sometimes she looked furious, then confused, then sad, and then a sudden a ray of bright joy would break and illuminate her whole face, making her more beautiful than I'd ever seen her.

I knew there was nothing I could do but wait. Inside me, there was a chaos of feelings about everything that had happened waiting to be dealt with, but right now I could ignore it all. Just knowing that about myself surprised me, but then, I had known all this would change me.

After what felt like hours, Mum finally opened her eyes. "Phew," she said, puffing out her cheeks. Pulling her shoulders back, she looked around us at the dark kitchen and shook her head. "It's gotten late." She leaned over to switched the light on. "Are you hungry?"

I watched her for a moment, then nodded.

"I'll make something – no, you stay there."

She held out a hand to stop me and I collapsed back into the chair, glad to not have to move.

"I'm honoured you've trusted me with this," she said, running the tap. "I can't lie, it was hard to hear some of it, but I'm glad you told me. Thank you."

"You're okay with it?" I asked. Was she this calm because she planned to take me back to the doctor? I wondered. Did she even believe me?

"I can't say I was okay with it all at first, no," she said. "But after a while, well, I sorted through it."

My stomach churned; this was the moment of truth. Would she still back me up now that she knew everything? She took a deep breath and turned to face me. "I believe you," she said. The relief that must have shown all over my face. "I do."

I sank back in the chair, feeling like all my breath had left me.

"I've always known stuff like this was out there," she went on. "I've seen too much evidence to not believe in it. I just didn't ever expect to find it in my own family."

She laughed, but her hands were shaking. I tried to get to my feet but my legs wobbled beneath me and I had to sit down again. She pointed at me. "I'm not happy about the effect it's having on you though," she said, sounding much more Mum-like. "You need to be able to go to school, to live a normal life as well. It's all very interesting and may be important to you, but you still have to live here, in this culture too. And it's not okay for it to make you ill."

I grinned. This was much more like what I'd expected; I was on familiar ground.

"I know," I said. "I think once this thing with the shadow is over, I'll feel much better."

I didn't know that was true, but I couldn't believe it would always make me feel so ill. How could anyone do it at all if that was the case?

Mum narrowed her eyes. "And that's another thing," she said, banging a pan down on the stove. "This shadow thing – what is it and what does it have to do with you anyway?"

If I knew that, I thought, this would be a whole lot easier.

"And why is it making you so tired?" she went on, talking to herself now. Then she turned back to face me again. "Do you think I could have a look at the journal?"

I stared at her, my brain sluggish. I had no idea; I hadn't asked Tierne. But he hadn't given me any caveats, and it wasn't like it had been locked or anything when we got it. I couldn't see what the harm was. I nodded, and she beamed at me.

"Great. Maybe I can figure this out for you."

"I don't think it works like that," I said. "So far, it's all been about me working it out myself."

She waved her hand at me over her shoulder. "Oh, I know," she said, sounding excited, "but there's no harm in trying is there? I might be able to help."

I shrugged; I couldn't see any reason for her not to try. It's not like the book was going to be any less cryptic for her than me.

Sleep was overwhelming me; I watched Mum cook dinner, unable to say anything while she chatted away. I could feel the relationship between us shifting, like sand dunes in a hurricane, and wondered how it would all work out in the end. But I couldn't worry about it anymore – I had no energy left for that.

I ate my dinner quickly, fighting to keep my eyes open and not look as tired as I felt. I could feel the dreaming coming on me; I had to get to bed before I collapsed. And in the long term, I told myself, I had to figure out how to control this.

By the time we'd finished and I could finally go upstairs, it was past 10'o'clock. Mum followed me, still beaming and fussing over me as I got ready for bed. As I climbed in beneath the covers, I pointed towards my desk drawer and caught her eye. She nodded at me, her eyes twinkling as she opened it and pulled out Grandma's red journal, holding it between both hands like something sacred.

She leaned over and kissed me on the forehead. My eyes closed, and I barely heard her tiptoe out of the room. Already, the waves of darkness were carrying me far from my body.

THIRTY

The house was quiet. Everything was bathed in a half-light as I padded down the stairs. Beneath my palm, the stair rail felt cool and smooth. My feet seemed to move with a grace they didn't normally have, making no sound at all, and through the open windows I could see only vague tree shapes waving with the wind.

Downstairs, the hallway was darker. I passed the kitchen door, feeling my way with my hands even though I knew each step by heart. The door to the living room stood half open and beyond it blossomed a warm, golden glow.

I glided towards it and reached my hand out. My fingers glimmered like moonlight as they pressed against the door, and for a moment I felt the pulse of sunlight and water running through me. I recognised the life of the tree hidden in dry wood.

Then the door swung open, revealing the living room beyond, and each object sang a story. I could smell desert dust in the Egyptian lamp, feel the warm damp of rainforest from the paintings on the wall; the books were like a choir. The whole room – the whole house – was alive around me; threads of feeling connected every object to its own history and I could know each one with a single glance.

I stepped further into the room and saw my mother on the sofa with Grandma's journal open in her lap. The soft light I had assumed was coming from a lamp radiated from her, illuminating the room. It danced through her skin like sunlight on water, stirring her clothes and hair like a breeze.

I stood and stared at her. I had never seen anything so beautiful in my whole life, not even out in the woods. Not even in the snowy forest of my dreams. I wanted to drink the sight of her.

She didn't look up at me. She seemed to be frozen, in fact, not moving apart from her steady, shallow breath. I took a step closer and bent over her. She still didn't move, and for the first time a shiver ran through me.

"Mum?" I whispered. The soft, peaceful emptiness I had been feeling, the threads of connection to every object around me, vanished.

The air around her was frigid; my breath hung in the air with each exhale. I bit my lip, trying to think. Was I dreaming? I whipped my head around; there was nothing but tree branches beyond the window, nothing but the sound of wind in the leaves around the house. No cars, no people —nothing but the silent hush of snow muffling everything.

Another shiver ran down my spine. How had I not realised I was dreaming? But I already knew the answer; it was so real, so solid beneath my hands and feet. Dreaming had become as real to me as my physical life. The realisation shocked me, and the shock brought warmth to my chest. I focused on that warmth for a few seconds, then shuffled closer to the sofa and bent down to look into Mum's face.

Her eyes were open and staring at the book in her hands

but they weren't moving; there was no light and no expression within them. She didn't look up at me or move at all as I crept closer.

I reached out a hand and brushed aside her fallen hair so I could see her better. It was like frozen silk in my hand; it burned my skin. I gasped and pulled away.

Somewhere deep within me, a voice spoke. It was harsh, like ice cracking in my mind, and it told me this was all my fault.

I stood up straight again. Go away, I told it, clenching my fists. Far away, somewhere out in the snow, I heard a wild laugh in reply. Cold drenched my skin and I had to fight to keep breathing. But it was different this time; at my core there was a warmth the ice couldn't touch. Heat burned there like fire, brighter with every moment, and I turned my mind towards it.

"Tierne," I whispered. This was the moment he had told me about. The shadow had come, and in my bones I knew that it had taken my mother.

"Tierne," I said again, a little louder, turning on the spot. A shiver went through the room. Like a curtain drawing back, it all dissolved around me. For one last moment, I saw the golden glow of my mother out of the corner of my eye and then she was gone as well. I was standing in the forest with my feet deep in the snow.

"Tierne!" My shriek echoed from tree to tree, making little drifts of snow fall from the branches. For a moment, nothing happened. Then a rumble ran through the ground beneath me – a sound like thunder that I felt more than heard – and through the trees the Great Bear paced towards me.

Relief flooded down from my heart into my arms and legs, overwhelming the cold that was quickly turning them numb. I ran towards him.

"Tierne," I whispered again, coming to a stop just in front

of his steaming muzzle. I wanted to reach out and run my hands through his rough fur, but I held in the impulse; he was a still a bear, after all.

"Little friend," he said, and his breath misted the cold air.

I bowed my head. "The shadow has taken my mother," I said, and saying it aloud made it more real, more true; my heart faltered and I fought back tears.

"It uses her as a lure," he said. He raised one enormous paw and used it to lift my chin so he could look into my face. "It works your fear and your guilt against you."

I nodded. But how did knowing that help me now?

"I have to find it, don't I?" I said, already knowing the answer. "And then what?" I forced myself to look into his fierce eyes. The fire inside my heart flared, filling me with warmth; I trusted him.

He swung his great head, gave me a long look, and said, "Follow me." Then he turned back to the trees and I stepped forward to walk beside him.

We moved like ghosts through the forest, making no sound. All around us, snow fell against the tree trunks. It seemed that the ground sped beneath my feet. I knew we were travelling very fast, and soon I was deeper in the forest than I had ever been before.

I looked up at Tierne beside me and he looked down at me.

"Where are we?" I whispered to him. Around us, the trees were thinner, black with what looked like ash smeared on their trunks, and the ground was darker too. It felt different to the forest I knew.

Tierne stopped. "The Hunting Grounds," he said, and I noticed that his breath didn't mist on the air like it had earlier. It was warmer here; there was less snow on the ground, and up ahead the vegetation was thicker. I wanted to ask him what the hunting grounds were, but it seemed wrong to break the thick silence between the trees. He swung his head low, caught my eye, and then turned ahead again. "Follow me closely," he told me over his shoulder.

I walked in his paw prints as much as I could, near enough to hold onto his fur if I'd had the courage. The trees crowded in around me and I thought I could hear them whispering in low murmurs as I passed. I swallowed; we were moving more slowly now, as though Tierne was picking his way along a hidden path. For the first time in the forest, I felt surrounded by eyes, and wondered who was here with us.

The ground was sloping downwards, becoming more muddy and slippery. I reached out a hand through the gloom to brace myself against a nearby tree and gasped. Just like in my house, the rough wood beneath my skin was breathing, pulsating with life like a real, physical tree. And deep beneath its bark I could feel the tides of memory flowing; the sunlight from the sky long ago that had helped it to grow, the route every particle of water had taken to reach its roots. The story of that tree was in my mind, almost louder than my own.

I pulled my hand away as though I'd been burnt and the connection lingered for a moment before fading. But now that I had felt it, I could recognise it all around me; the voices, the eyes I'd been feeling were the trees themselves, all alive, all aware of my passage between them.

Tierne glanced over his shoulder at me, waiting for a moment before continuing. I stumbled after him, slipping on the wet ground but making sure I didn't touch any more trees. My heart was pounding; everything I touched or saw was alive – it spoke and sang to me, and I wondered how I had ever missed it.

Tierne led me deeper and deeper downward until the banks

of earth seemed to encircle us, cutting off almost all of the light. I forced down the growing panic about where Mum was and what could be happening to her. Thinking about that wasn't going to help.

At last, we reached the bottom of the slope and the trees opened up around us to form a shadowy glade. The branches here were even more ragged. They entangled and snared one another as they reached upward, blocking off most of the sky, and in the centre of the space was a wide pool of dark water. I shivered and wrapped my arms tightly around me, then followed Tierne as he took a path around the boundary of the glade.

I could feel the trees crowding around me like people. I could feel them in my mind and pressing against my skin, making it hard to breathe. I felt dizzy, almost jostled; there were so many of them, so many voices. I ran a hand across my forehead and it came away covered in sweat. Ahead of me, Tierne was waiting at the bottom of the slope; I had fallen behind.

I pushed the voices away, trying to listen to the steady pulse of my heart. But my feet were slipping on the mud and it was harder and harder to breathe. A wave of nausea ran through me, and out of the corner of my eye I thought I saw something move. My head whipped around, my whole body humming with tension. I stared at the glassy surface of the pool.

I couldn't look away. There was nothing to see, but my eyes were caught. I couldn't move. And then a sick ripple of horror ran through me, echoing the ripple that broke the surface of the pool.

I could only stare. Something was emerging from the water. Low and shapeless with no features, it hauled itself out of the water and onto the mud. I wanted to scream, but my throat had squeezed shut. The fire inside my chest shrank back as a thick, stagnant smell pressed against my skin. I was weak with nausea as it reached out a dripping limb towards me.

There was a blur, huge and dark in front of me, and I closed my eyes. My knees buckled and I felt like the darkness would overwhelm me. A shriek filled the clearing and then a terrifying roar rocked the ground.

There was a moment of silence, and I pressed my eyes even more tightly closed. Tierne's smoky breath encircled me.

"Little one." His voice was like a light in the shadows. I swam back to him through the torrent of voices that were pressing into me. I felt his warm breath on my cheek and a single, soft brush of his fur against my chest as he touched me with his snout, and I opened my eyes.

"Keep moving," he said. He turned and walked beside me as I staggered out of the clearing.

The moment we crossed the line of trees, the pressure inside me eased and I could breathe again. I gasped, bending over and shivering as the cold, clear air flooded into my lungs again. Tierne waited a few seconds, then started up the slope and I forced my legs to follow him.

We walked on, and at times I wondered how it could still be night time in the real world. I was tired – so tired that my limbs felt like stone. I stopped thinking about any of it. The world had become this slow, careful tramp up the frosty slope, and I pressed on after him.

Just as I thought the last of the light was leaving me and I would be walking in that half-darkness forever, the slope leveled off. We broke out of the trees on to snowy plain. The sudden whiteness of it all was blinding and I had to shade my eyes with my hands as freezing air bit into my face.

At last, Tierne stopped. He turned to me, his legs deep in

the banks of snow and his fur sparkling with ice. I waited for him to speak.

He said, "We're close."

Nothing stirred as he broke the silence. Behind me, I could feel the ranks of trees watching us. Ahead, the white plain went on forever and above us the sky was low and heavy with clouds shrouding the moon. I wrapped my arms around myself as a cold wind bored into my chest. I thought Tierne was going to speak again, but he just stood there, a massive warmth beside me.

"What was that place?" I asked. I didn't have to explain what I meant.

Out of the corner of my eye, the forest was like a dark wall. There was only the faintest glimmer of moonlight between the shadowy branches, and I knew that somewhere back there was that terrible pool. Would we have to pass it again to get home?

Tierne shifted in the snow. "That was the Hunting Grounds," he told me again.

I blew warm air into my hands and rubbed them together, watching him. The burning light was growing brighter inside me again now that we were out of the trees, and I felt much more like myself.

"But what does that mean?"

He huffed, and he bared his teeth in a fierce grin. I wondered if he was angry or amused. "It is the place where lost souls wait," he told me.

"Lost souls?"

"Souls that have died but have no home to go to." I could feel his eyes examining me, gauging my reaction. "Or are too afraid to go there."

I thought about it. "Kind of like limbo?"

He shrugged his enormous shoulders. "In a way."

I tried to repress the urge to glance over my shoulder again. Knowing what it was didn't make it any less creepy. "What are they waiting for?"

"Someone to lead them home," he said, then added, "or nothing – most of them have forgotten why they're there."

"And what was in the pool?"

His nostrils flared. "Something dark," he said, "and hungry." I wanted to ask more, but he interrupted me. "We are wasting time."

He lifted his head to look out across the plain and I dragged my thoughts from the dark forest behind me to follow his gaze. I knew why I'd been stalling; out there, somewhere, was the fear I had to face. The shadow and my mother. And after the long walk to get there, I was wishing we had further to go.

The fire inside me flared, pushing aside the freezing numbness in my face and legs. I knew the direction I had to take like a magnet knows north. There was no point feeling scared or uncertain now, I tried to tell myself, focusing on the great bulk of Tierne beside me. He had saved me at the pool and he would save me again, if needed.

I hoped I was right.

"What do I have to do?" I asked. Snow was just beginning to spiral down from the clouds, making the landscape hazy.

"Find them."

The heat inside me swirled, calling for me to follow it. I took a step, and then another, watching to see if Tierne agreed. But he simply watched, giving me no indication that I was going the right way. This was, then, another of those things I had to do for myself.

I turned from him and lifted my chin. I could do this. The fire inside me was bright and I knew my mum was out there, glowing with the same light. I stepped through the falling snowflakes, my feet sinking nearly a foot into the snow with each step, and headed in the direction that felt the warmest. Behind me, I heard Tierne follow.

The snow was firm and tiring to walk through. Beneath it lay a glassy layer of ice, and I realised with a jolt that we were standing on a frozen lake, not a plain of grass. Beneath my feet, if I concentrated, I could feel the expanse of water; the reeds, the fish, the currents. They sang on the edge of my awareness, just like the trees in the Hunting Grounds had.

The ice beneath the snow was thick. It was silent as we walked across it, even with Tierne's huge weight, and I realised it must be metres deep. Reassured, I moved faster.

The snow swirled around me more and more thickly, becoming a blinding vortex only to part and reveal nothing but more whiteness. There was no light ahead, and no shadow, but I was walking quickly now, confident in the direction I was taking. With every step, the feeling got stronger and stronger until it felt like I was filling with fire.

Then I was running, and Tierne was like thunder behind me. I had seen them; I knew it. A glimpse of movement and colour, shadow and form, through the snow.

I raced to where I'd seen them, batting snowflakes out of my way. I was certain this was the place, but there was nothing. Tierne came to stand beside me. He swung his head around, taking in the emptiness of the spot. "You saw something?"

"Right here."

He padded in a circle, sniffing the snow. Then he drew a claw across the ice beneath us and gulped the air with a huge smacking sound. I watched him as my heartbeat slowed.

"They are here," he said at last, turning to face me.

I stared up into his soft face and breathed in the smell of his fur as he came closer. "But where?"

"Close your eyes."

I obeyed. I could feel him so close to me that his warmth mixed with mine. In my mind's eye, I could see the rich texture of his fur, so many reds and browns and golds with a dusting of silver snow. He was so close that I could feel his breath on my neck.

I stood as still as I could and waited, forcing myself to keep my eyes closed.

"Can you still feel them?" he asked in a low growl. I nodded.

They were here; I knew it. My eyes couldn't see them but my heart could. Its light radiated into the space around us and it told me what my other senses couldn't know. Here, right in this space, the shadow was hiding with my mother. I nodded again.

"Reach out with your feeling," he whispered right into my ear. A shiver ran down my spine. I knew what he meant at once. I reached out for them, feeling for the exact point where they were hidden. I could feel them both as clearly as if I were seeing them in front of me: two distinct songs in the darkness, one dark, one golden. I braced myself for the shadow to fight me, but nothing happened.

"Good," Tierne said. "Now show me."

I hesitated, but I knew what he wanted me to do. There was no reason to doubt myself now. I took a breath, and the snowflakes in the air melted the moment they touched my lips. With my lungs full, I poured the feeling from my heart into my breath. Then I let it go.

The breath flowed out of my mouth and into Tierne's face, and I felt him suck it in like smoke. His fur tickled my face and snagged on my hair; he was so close, I could have rested my forehead against his jaw. I waited and wondered what we had to do, gently holding onto the feeling of the shadow and my mum like a beacon.

But before Tierne could tell me, I knew. It was as though I'd always known. I reached out with my hands into the space around me, and it was like there was a pathway in the air for them to follow. The warm light from my centre poured along my arms, and Tierne stepped back to give me more space. I thought of Grandma, and my Great Grandmother, and all the other women who had done this before me.

I reached out with my hands of light into the darkness around me. No snow was falling on me now; the icy lake was almost gone, just an echo beyond the beat of my heart. I felt for the place where they stood as delicately as I could so I wouldn't reveal myself too soon. I took a final breath, feeling it stoke the flames within me, and then the golden fire flowed down through my arms and legs, through my mind, out of my hands, and I reached across the last few inches and took hold of them both.

A scream tore through the darkness around me as the shadow writhed, but my mother was still in my hand and I grasped her arm as she sank to the ground. Somewhere, far away, I heard Tierne huff and felt his weight shake the earth as he moved forward, but I couldn't pay attention to him. The shadow was pulling, twisting in my grip, trying to escape, and I held it tighter. A laugh ran through me for a moment as I realised what I was doing. Only a few days ago, the thought of touching this thing would have frozen me with horror.

But none of that mattered now. I knew, in the same way I had known where it was hiding, that it belonged to me. It couldn't escape me forever, and it couldn't harm me as long as I held it tight.

"Come back," I heard Tierne whisper in my ear, and for a moment I didn't know what he meant. His fur brushed my cheek as he whispered to me again. I tightened my grip on the shadow, I opened my eyes and came back to the cold lake.

There it was, like a dark stain on the air in front of me. My mother was motionless on the ground a few feet away, but I ignored her. There was nothing I could do for her yet.

I stared into the darkness of the shadow, awed at how strange and solid it was. It had given up fighting. Out of the corner of my eye, I saw Tierne bend over Mum's body and sniff her. She would be all right, I told myself, but my attention was broken. A grain of fear niggled at the back of my mind and I tried to push it away.

The shadow loomed and stretched, pulling against my grasp. It reached upward, swelling like a cloud as the light and warmth inside me faltered. I clung to it and tried to force myself to brighten again, but the kernel of fear was there and it was growing.

The shadow grinned at me with its jagged mouth. It was getting stronger and taller by the moment. I shook my head, trying to get rid of its voice in my mind. What if she doesn't wake up again? It will be all your fault, it said. A pit of horror opened in my stomach. Doubt filled me; I didn't know what to do.

You looked into the pool, it said, you wasted time in the forest, you gave her the journal that let it in — you, you you, it crooned at me, and I pressed my free hand to my ear.

"Stop it," I said, and it laughed. The light inside me was shrinking, fading as the shadow leaned over me, pressing its blank, frozen face close to mine. Behind it, Tierne was standing over my mother with his teeth bared; now I knew the difference between his smile and his snarl. There was no mistaking the power in his face, the threat of those teeth.

But they couldn't help me now; I knew it was too late. I had touched the shadow, I had taken hold of it, and now I couldn't let go. There was nothing Tierne could do.

Despair flooded me. I'm sorry, I thought, seeing the faces of everyone I'd ever let down. Sandy, Milly, Mum, my friends, even my dad. And Grandma – I could see her sad face, disappointed with me and my failure, shaking her head and turning away from me.

A pain ached down my throat like a cramp, choking me.

The shadow shivered and its arms came up to grab me. I stared into the abyss of its mouth, wondering what it would be like to be eaten. My whole body was wracked with the pain of my failure. It beat like a hammer on my heart, in my lungs, through my blood, and I gasped, feeling as though I would burst apart at any moment.

The shadow stalled, frozen in mid-air. Looking down at myself, I forgot all about it. The raw pain met my brightness and they strained against each other. Beneath my skin, my arms, legs, fingers and torso writhed as the two forces intertwined. Then my body began to crack.

Within moments, I was in a hundred pieces. They fell away like ash as the fire inside me exploded; golden flames spilled into the snowy air, sparking with rainbow shards. I laughed. My body was gone; where my arms and legs had been there were now limbs of light.

The snow around me began to melt, turning to water that spread across the ice. I looked up with my new eyes to where the shadow waited. My shining hand was still tight around its twisting arm and it lurched and pulled against me. I smiled.

I stepped towards it, pulling it close and looking deep into its empty eyes. I felt the light within me swell like a wave and I took another step, into the shadow itself. I felt its darkness fill me for a moment, then it swirled and disintegrated into dust with a soft hiss.

I breathed it in, pulling it into every part of me. There was no world but light.

Then I sighed and the world returned.

THIRTY-ONE

I looked up and met Tierne's eyes. He was the only dark shape in a world of white and blue, and beneath his body lay my mother. I stared at her for a few seconds before the reality of what had happened flooded through me.

I ran forward and knelt beside her, taking one of her hands in mine. It was light and warm, but almost transparent.

"Will she be okay?"

Tierne huffed and stepped away, showering her with snow. "She will be fine," he said.

Tears stung my eyes. Looking down at my hands, I realised that I was flesh and blood once more. "What do I do now?"

He pressed his muzzle into her open palm then said, "Send her home."

I hesitated. The strange being of light who had taken my place for a moment was gone, along with all of her certainty.

"You know how," he told me.

I lifted her shoulders awkwardly and slipped my other hand beneath knees. She was so light that I could stand with her in my arms. Closing my eyes, I saw the sofa in our warm living room, and her lying on it, asleep. I took a deep breath, feeling for that place as strongly as I could and allowing it to fill my lungs. Then I blew into her face. In my arms, I felt the lightness of her grow even lighter, until it was gone.

I opened my eyes. She had vanished; I had sent her home on my breath.

I rose to stand in the snow, giddy with relief and half laughing at myself. My feet skidded on the ice and I reached out to steady myself against Tierne, who was warm and solid under my hands. Then a wave of exhaustion hit me and I sagged against him.

The journey back through the forest was like the memory of a dream; the smell of Tierne's fur against my face, his wide back rocking beneath me as I clung to his shoulders. I don't know how long it took or what path he followed, but eventually we were back between familiar trees and looking out over the rolling hills of snow as I rested against him.

"This is a good start," Tierne said, his breath like smoke in the air.

I had just enough strength left to groan at the thought. "Will it always be this hard?"

He shrugged. I looked into his wild face and realised that he was smiling at me. And then he breathed on me and the darkness hit me like a tidal wave.

THIRTY-TWO

I woke with the first light on Tuesday morning. For the slightest moment, I wondered if I was still dreaming. I heard movement downstairs, then a car passed outside my window. I was home.

I slipped out of bed, feeling strange and heavy in my solid body. The carpet beneath my toes was soft. The room was more colourful that I'd ever noticed before. Everything was new, as though the whole world had been reborn. And for the first time in what seemed like years, I felt awake, full of clarity and light. All the tiredness had gone.

Mum was sitting in the kitchen when I got downstairs, sipping a cup of tea as she watched the sun creep into our garden. Grandma's journal lay on the table in front of her. It was closed.

She turned to meet my eyes as I walked into the room and for a moment all I could see was the radiant gold glow from my dream. Then the vision vanished and she was my mum again; a bit pale, with dark rings under her eyes. She gestured for me to sit down with her.

"How are you feeling?" I asked.

"The strangest thing happened last night."

"Oh yeah? What was that?"

She narrowed her eyes. "Why don't you tell me?" she said, taking another sip of tea. I sighed. It was only fair that she should know. I just hoped she wouldn't freak out too much.

So I told her everything. Everything apart from how she'd looked in my dream – I thought that could wait for another time. I told her how the shadow had used the journal to pull her into the forest and hide her. How Tierne and I had tracked them both down and sent her home. How the shadow had vanished.

She sat and listened in rapt silence, drinking in every word. It was only when I got to the end and sat staring at her, waiting for her reaction, that she looked down at the journal, just laying there on the table.

"It matches everything..." She looked up at me. "I remember all of that, just how you explained," she said, her face pale. "I thought it was a nightmare, but then you appeared with that bear, and..." She shook her head, staring at me. "It's true," she whispered. Her eyes were shining with tears, but she wasn't freaked out, I realised. She was glad.

"I think you'd better take this back," she said, pointing at the journal. "I'm so excited, Anne," she added. "This is so exciting!"

I laughed. "I'm glad you feel that way," I said as I slid the journal across the table and into my lap. "Because I don't think I can go back now."

THIRTY-THREE

"What do you think happened to the shadow?" Milly asked. We were huddled together in our coats and scarves, watching the stream pass by at our feet. It had only been a few weeks since we'd been out there together in the last of the summer sunshine, but the trees were already turning golden. I reached forward, dropped a fallen leaf into the swirling water, then watched it dance away.

"I don't really understand it up here," I said at last, tapping my temple.

"I think it was part of you all along," she said.

I let the idea sink into me. It made no rational sense at all, but I was used to that by now. It felt right though.

"So what are you doing with Tierne now?" she asked.

I snorted. "I'm insisting on a break."

Milly leaned back on her arms to look at me.

"But he says we'll be talking to Grandma a lot soon," I said. "She's got stuff to teach me," I added. "Do you want the journal back?"

"No thanks. I've been talking to Grandma myself lately," she said.

"Really, how?"

She shrugged. "I just... listen," she said, catching my eye. I nodded; she didn't ever have to worry about me not believing her.

We sat for a while longer, not saying anything. The stream was singing to us, and behind me the woods rustled their story, making me think of the white forest. I would go back there soon. Maybe tonight, I thought, smiling to myself.

AUTHOR'S NOTE

This story is totally fictional, but it is drawn from my own experiences in working with ancient shamanic teachings. There's no really flashy magic in the story of The Forest, because all of the magic that's in it is real - it's comprised of experiences and tools that we can actually use, from using dreams to meet with teachers and ancestors, to scrying in internet text.

If you'd like to know more about some of the methods used in this book in a friendly, step by step way, you can find details in The Way of Change: Finding Your Power To Thrive In A Changing World - by me!

At the back of this book I've also included a list of some excellent non-fiction books that you can use to learn more about these amazing traditions. And if you'd like to read more stories featuring these kinds of magic, you can **sign up to my newsletter**.

If you enjoyed this book, please give me the only gift an author ever dreams of - a review.

Thank you!

ABOUT THE AUTHOR

Luitha lives in the UK with contemporary artist <u>Gabriel Tamaya</u> and their four small trolls.

Her writing includes fiction, mostly supernatural, fantasy, horror and sci-fi all mixed together; poetry, mostly mystical; and non-fiction, mostly about shamanism.

You can email her at **luitha@lktamaya.co.uk**

She will email back. But she can't guarantee her reply won't be covered in troll slime and 10 years late due to a fey-induced time vortex.

Luitha's Blog is at lktamaya.co.uk

Luitha's on Twitter at twitter.com/LKTamaya

And Luitha's on Pinterest at pinterest.com/lktamaya

READING LIST

Prehistoric Belief: Shamans, Trance and the Afterlife by Mike Williams

Shaman Pathways: Elen of the Ways by Elen Sentier

The Spirits Are Always With Me: True Stories and Guidance From A Modern Shaman by Jane Shutt

Shaman, Healer, Sage by Alberto Villoldo